Squad Six Series
Bound by Valor
Bound by Thorns
Bound by Scars
Bound by Ruin

Bound by Valor

BAKUL SHARMA

Copyright © 2024 by Bakul Sharma

Cover Design by ANKBookDesigns

Editing by Roxana Coumans

All rights reserved.

No part of this publication may be reproduced, distributed, or transmitted in any form or by any means, including photocopying, recording, or other electronic or mechanical methods, without the prior written permission of the publisher, except as permitted by Canadian copyright law. For permission requests, contact Bakul Sharma at bakul@authorbakulsharma.com.

The story, all names, characters, and incidents portrayed in this production are fictitious. No identification with actual persons (living or deceased), places, buildings, and products is intended or should be inferred.

1st edition 2024

ISBN ebook: 978-1-0689938-0-0

ISBN paperback: 978-1-0689938-1-7

PLAYLIST

Shameless
Camila Cabello

Flames
R3HAB, ZAYN & Jungleboi

Next to Me
Imagine Dragons

Centuries
Fall Out Boy

Beige
Yoke Lore

MONTAGEM CORAL
DJ Holanda, MC GW, and MC TH

Brother
Kodaline

Rose
Honest Men

CONTENT WARNING

This book contains themes and scenes that may be triggering for some readers. It features explicit sexual content, as well as an obsessive, protective, and sometimes controlling hero with stalking behavior towards the heroine.

Trigger Warnings:
Violence
Kidnapping
Blood
Murder
Grief
Stalking
Mentions of physical assault
Mentions of death
Mentions of slavery
Mentions of human trafficking

Welcome to Squad Six!

DEDICATION

For every woman who's ever dreamed of kicking ass in heels or combat boots.

ONE

Leora

He was dead.

Good.

A deep, dark part of me wished I had been the one to end Adriano, not some faceless thug in prison. The main reason I had accepted the Resident Psychologist position at the Toronto South Detention Centre instead of the northern one was him; he was locked up there. The irony of it was biting, cruel almost.

As I stared at the email from my lawyer confirming his death, a swirl of relief and regret churned inside me. This should have been good news—freedom from a past that haunted me. Yet, there lingered a gnawing desire, a primal wish that I had been the one to kill him. Wasn't that how all women felt about their exes?

Maybe not.

My train of thought was interrupted by the buzz of my phone. I always kept it silent, a habit ingrained during my time with Adriano. He despised hearing it ring at night. Looking back, his rage over such trivial things should have been a red flag.

I watched my phone, vibrating in my hand, with 'Mom' flashing on the screen. Staring, frozen, I let it buzz through until it slipped into voicemail.

An hour later, I walked into my gym and greeted the coach with a nod before diving into my warm-up routine. It was a regular intermediate kickboxing class, one I had been attending for the past year.

Was I getting any better?

Probably.

Did I actively use MMA to release my pent-up rage?

Absolutely.

It wasn't just a hobby; it was a necessity, a vital release. The ghost of Adriano clung to me, a relentless shadow darkening every moment of peace I might find. The weight on my chest felt unshakable. This weight, this ever-present pressure on my chest, seemed immovable.

So, I embraced the brutal rhythm of MMA. There was a twisted irony in it. I'd felt the sting of blows before, the memories lost to the fog of trauma-induced amnesia.

What a fucking blessing!

My body knew, even if my mind refused to remember. Each strike I landed reverberated back to me, echoing off the gym walls. Every punch thrown felt like justice, a declaration of strength I had once believed stripped from me.

I didn't linger after class; I made a beeline for the exit, eager to leave the sweat and exertion behind. The subway ride home was as nondescript as any other, but once I emerged, a spontaneous decision steered me off my usual path. I needed a smoke—a quick detour to the convenience store seemed harmless enough.

There are moments where your life takes a turn. When the monotonous, fluid rhythm of your days morphs into something rigid and eventually breaks, leaving you to deal with the scatter.

I didn't realize it then, but that detour was about to cost me.

As I neared the store, the air grew tense. From the dark alley beside the store, voices clashed—a sharp, fraught exchange that sliced through the night's calm.

"Don't fucking move," came a man's frustrated voice.

"I'm not moving, but are you sure you want to kill me?" another man replied, his voice strained and weary. A chill ran through my veins.

It was 11:30 PM in a shady part of Toronto, and the night was darker than usual. Despite being accustomed to hearing about violence, encountering it firsthand in this grim alley still sent a shiver through me. As I cautiously peered around the corner, two men stood menacingly over a dark-haired man sprawled on the ground, clutching his stomach. The attackers, their backs to me, were caught up in a heated interrogation.

"Who sent you?" the one with blonde hair demanded.

"You tell me. I'm not the one responsible for

random security hacks in the financial district," the injured man said.

"He's a fucking narc. I told you!" his companion with a buzz cut shouted.

I was about to dial 911 when my phone vibrated with an incoming message.

Startled, I looked up just in time to see the two men turning their gaze towards me. Dropping my gym bag to the side, I braced myself, ready for what might come next. Boxing had taught me well—I knew how to throw a punch: straight, uppercut, shuffle, hook. With my hands still wrapped from class, I felt oddly prepared and grateful for it.

As the blond man advanced towards me, adrenaline surged. I picked up my pace, leaped against the wall to gain height over the six-foot assailant, and delivered a forceful kick right to his jaw. The impact sent his knife skittering away across the alley.

The news about Adriano had been gnawing at me. Although part of me felt justice had been served, another part was frustrated—deeply frustrated. I hadn't been the one to end his torment on me. Tonight, as I stood in this alley, every nerve in my body was primed, every muscle coiled. I really needed to kick someone's ass today. It was more than self-defense; it was a necessary catharsis that no amount of punching bags or controlled sparring could ever provide.

"This bitch," the buzz cut hissed, his voice echoing off the grimy alley walls.

Out of the corner of my eye, I caught the injured dark-haired man smirking, even as he clutched at a wound I couldn't quite see. Driven by adrenaline, I delivered a swift uppercut followed by a hook, then shuffled to his leading side to land a solid punch right in his gut. He was so unprepared—clearly not a boxer—that he didn't even attempt to block.

As I was about to throw another punch, Blondie grabbed my braided hair and yanked me back toward him. Reacting instinctively, I spun around, pivoting off the pull, and grabbed him by the neck, delivering a sloppy but effective knee to his nose. I glanced over, expecting Buzz Cut to jump into the fray, but found him on the ground, the dark-haired man now surprisingly upright and active.

"I got this," he declared, hurling a knife so close it nearly grazed me, likely finding its mark in Blondie.

Within seconds, the alley was empty except for us, Blondie and Buzz Cut stumbling away with a trail of curses. My hands shook with the intensity of the encounter. My nerves shot. The dark-haired man let out a chuckle, his deep voice annoyingly calm in the aftermath.

He's laughing?

"Excuse me? I think you owe me an explanation. And a thank you wouldn't hurt," I scoffed, my frustration palpable.

He approached slowly, closing the distance until he towered over me. His hands gently gripped my shoulders, nudging me into the streetlight. He brushed his knuckles softly against my cheek, his voice low and steady, "They cut you."

The light hit his face just right, illuminating the powerful lines of his jaw shadowed by the light stubble. His tanned skin caught the yellow glow of the streetlight, his dark eyes shimmering with a golden intensity. He was, unexpectedly, the most striking man I'd ever seen.

It took a moment for his words to register. Instinctively, my hands flew to my cheek, coming away with traces of blood. Nothing, though, compared to the dark-haired man's hands, soaked through with it.

"Did you get stabbed?" I asked, my voice shaky from the adrenaline still coursing through me.

He glanced nonchalantly at his belly. His black shirt underneath his jacket was drenched and shining with slick blood. "I guess, yeah."

"Do you live nearby?" he asked, scanning the intersection.

"Y-yes," I managed, my reply faltering.

"Good. We're going to your place."

"Wait, what?" The words tumbled out before I could think.

"Don't you want to finish saving me? I thought that's why you were flying around kicking ass."

His words hung in the air, laced with a half-mocking challenge. For a moment, I hesitated, torn. Was I really considering taking a bloodied stranger to my home? The thought spun around in my mind, wrestling with the adrenaline still pumping through my veins. How irresponsible could I be in a single night? Yet, there he stood, smirking as if he'd already known I'd say yes, his presence a strange and sudden weight in my life. The decision teetered on the edge of recklessness. Could I walk away?

My hesitant laugh broke through, betraying my nerves, yet my voice was steady as I replied, "Sure, damsel. Let's get you patched up."

There was a flicker of amusement, perhaps surprise, in his eyes at my agreement. He nodded, gesturing for me to take the lead, and followed me as we made our way to my apartment.

TWO

Zarek

Stepping further into her apartment, my gaze darted to a small urn and a portrait of a charming cat perched atop a bookshelf.

"I'm sorry about," I leaned in to read the name inscribed on the urn, "Ada."

She shot me a look of mild amusement and commanded, "Take off your jacket."

"We're not—" I began, but my words faltered as she shrugged off her denim jacket and draped it over a chair by the kitchen island. Beneath the jacket, her figure was unexpectedly striking—tall, slender, yet defined in all the right places. The jacket had concealed much more than I expected, including the pert little ass she'd been hiding in those cargo pants. Despite the stabbing pain in my gut, a different heat flared within me.

"Whatever you're thinking, stop. I need to check that wound," she interjected, snapping me back to the present. Needless to say, her confidence was unshaken. If only she knew who she let into her apartment.

She vanished into what appeared to be the bathroom and returned clutching a first aid kit and a damp towel. I reluctantly shed my jacket, wincing as the fabric moved over the fresh gash—a painful reminder of my underestimation back in the alley. I should've known there were two perps.

Carefully, I placed my jacket on the floor to avoid staining her belongings and eased myself onto the couch.

"May I?" she asked politely, her fingers poised to lift my shirt. As she began to gently clean the wound, her brow furrowed in concentration, capturing my full attention.

"You do this often?" I asked.

"What? Bring home injured men and clean up after them?" she chuckled and I decided that it was the best sound I had heard all day.

"What's your name?" I asked.

"Leora." She said softly.

Leora.

Suddenly, she was all I could see. My heart started running a million beats a minute. Her name was as beautiful as her, striking in a way that captured you, enamored you, *ruined* you. The glow of her tawny skin set against her dark braids gave her the aura of a warrior goddess—both my doom and my salvation wrapped into one.

What the fuck is going on with me?

"I'm Zarek," I blurted out, the words tumbling out before I could clamp down on the impulse. Stupid, revealing my real name, but the confession was already hanging between us. "I thought you should know, given you sort of saved my life back there."

"Sort of?" she quirked an eyebrow, pausing.

"Yeah, when you were handling the other guy, the first one tried to attack you with a knife. I stopped him." I angled my face towards her and smiled. "I guess we both owe each other a thank you."

"Well, thank you," she murmured softly, her focus returning to the wound. She wiped away the last of the blood with practiced ease, her expression unreadable.

What kind of a woman doesn't flinch over a stab wound?

She was an enigma. Her body was taut the entire time, coiled like a spring. Her high alert was understandable—I was, after all, a stranger who had barged into her life. Yet, I couldn't bring myself to leave. Hell, why was I even here? There was something about her, a pull that seemed to beckon me closer.

I was drawn to her, compelled to stay and unravel the mystery of the woman who had unexpectedly saved me.

"I think this needs stitches. I'm not qualified for that, neither do I have equipment," she said.

"It's fine. We can just bandage it up. I'll get medical attention tomorrow."

She carefully bandaged the wound and then gently pulled my t-shirt back down. "You shouldn't keep this t-shirt on; it's wet, and it's cold outside."

"Oh, I'm not planning on going anywhere tonight. But I wouldn't mind borrowing a woman's t-shirt for the night," I said with a smile.

She squinted her eyes. "Who are you, really?"

"I told you, I'm Zarek," I responded, trying to maintain a neutral expression.

"Why were you stabbed in the middle of an alley?"

"Wasn't it because I was chasing the two men you so bravely saved me from?"

"Don't play dumb. Tell me why. Should I be scared of you?" Her gaze was intense, probing, and though her face was stoic, I caught the flicker of fear in her eyes—a fear I knew I had caused.

"I'm not here to hurt you, Leora," I said, reaching slowly for my wallet to not startle her. She flinched slightly, watching my every move. I pulled out my police badge—a decoy issued by my team for interactions with civilians.

She inhaled sharply and whispered, "So you *are* a narc then."

"I'm in law enforcement, not a narc. What about you? I did just witness you assaulting two men."

"I'm pretty sure I deserve a badge of my own now," she laughed and I realized I was wrong before. *This* was the best sound I had heard all day, hell all *year!*

She excused herself to wash her hands and vanished into her bedroom through the adjoining bathroom. When she returned with a large T-shirt, a pang of curiosity struck me. It was a men's T-shirt. Did she have a boyfriend? Why was I even concerned?

"Here," she tossed it to me nonchalantly.

"Whose is this?" I couldn't help but ask.

"Jealous?" she teased with a smile. "It's mine. I prefer men's clothing."

I nodded, feigning indifference, yet a wave of relief washed over me.

Knock it off, Zar!

I quickly changed into the T-shirt she provided,

tossing my blood-soaked shirt atop my jacket. When I turned around, I caught Leora watching me intently. Had she observed me changing? I hadn't exactly hidden myself. A smirk appeared on my face, prompting her to roll her eyes dramatically.

"'Like what you see?'" she mocked in a deep voice.

"I wasn't going to say that," I chuckled.

"Oh please! You know you're hot. No need to pretend you're not flirting with your body."

Her voice echoed in my head as she called me out. I stood there, regretting my forwardness. I was usually more cautious, given the dangerous edges of my job. But there I was, right in her space, unintentionally sending all the wrong—or maybe the right—signals. This wasn't me, or at least it shouldn't have been.

I had to clear the air, fast. "Listen, I understand this situation is unusual, but I assure you, I'm not flirting with you with my body—or flirting at all."

The moment the words left my mouth, her expression dropped to one of embarrassment. I immediately regretted the sharpness in my tone. I hadn't meant to come across so harshly. But the damage was done.

"Uh, I'll head to bed. The spare room is that way."

She gestured and retreated to her bedroom so swiftly, I didn't get a chance to explain further.

THREE

Leora

He was gone by morning, leaving my door unlocked and a lingering embarrassment in the air after his pointed comment. It had made me second-guess every interaction—had I imagined the flirtation, or was it just wishful thinking?

Stranger equals danger, Leora. Get a grip!

With a sigh, I pulled my French press from the cabinet, my motions mechanical as I set about brewing my morning coffee. Today weighed heavy on me; I was summoned back to the interrogation rooms at the Detention Center. Though I'd be shielded behind reinforced glass, the proximity to condemned criminals on death row, unnerved me.

I poured the steaming coffee into my to-go mug and set out for the center. The building loomed over me as I approached, its stark, imposing structure feeling particularly oppressive under today's gray skies.

My appointment today was with Delara Booth

from Blackthorn Security, who was running the interrogation. The scant information I had been given mentioned an inmate tangled in a human trafficking ring, now turned scapegoat by his own crew. No doubt, Ms. Booth intended to exploit his precarious position, perhaps to flip his allegiance. The thought of what awaited made the coffee in my hand feel even colder.

After my usual checkin routine, I found myself sitting behind the glass, alongside Ms. Booth who was agitatedly tapping away on her phone.

"We were told you'd be joining us." She spoke in her posh British accent without looking up.

"Ah yes, Ms. Booth. I'm the resident psychologist for this Center. Happy to help you through this interrogation."

I cowered under her scrutinizing gaze, as she spoke again. "We technically don't need you, but I hear the inmate is pretty unstable. We might need you to calm him down."

I bristled slightly, correcting her, "My role doesn't include direct interaction, Ms. Booth. I'm here to observe and analyze body language and truthfulness. Direct contact with the inmate isn't part of the protocol I was briefed on."

"Well, aren't you useless, then?" She scoffed.

"Excuse me?" I countered.

"I said we don't need you. You'll be pretty bored giving absolutely no help for this."

"It's policy–"

She cut me off. "Fuck policy, Ms. Leora Mateez. We don't need you here unless it's to calm him down."

My anger bubbled over. "It's *Doctor* Leora Mateez. And what you're demanding is against our policy."

She rolled her fucking eyes at me and sighed dismissively. "Fine. Be here. But don't utter a single word, Ms. Mateez."

Her tone stung, but I clenched my jaw and shot back, "It's *doctor*, you bitch. Call me miss again, and I will end this interrogation before it even starts."

She smirked, clearly amused by my irritation, and sauntered out of the room. I was left fuming, my day already soured by Zarek's thoughts and now this encounter. Ms. Booth was really testing my limits.

The interrogation session passed without a hitch, much to my relief. Ms. Booth emerged from the room with a particularly triumphant air, her demeanor unnervingly cheery compared to her earlier frostiness. I provided her with my notes and let her be. Once I wrapped up my duties for the day, I made my way to the gym, eager to shake off the tension.

As I started my workout, I realized I was hitting the punching bag harder than usual. The day's frustrations were bleeding into each strike; I wasn't just practicing—I was venting. The memory of my recent scuffles with those thugs, Blondie and Buzzcut, crept into my mind. Oddly enough, I found myself missing the raw, chaotic energy of that very real fight.

Back then, every punch felt like shaking off chains. Now, facing the predictable rhythm of a regular sparring session, everything seemed too tame, too controlled. The gym was supposed to be my escape, but today it fell short of satisfying the craving for a real challenge that had ignited within me.

Dragging myself home, exhaustion clung to me like a second skin. Stepping off the train station and onto the bustling street, I caught a fleeting glimpse of a figure shrouded in black. His face was barely visible, but I knew his gaze was locked on me. The person momentarily slipped from view, then reappeared, walking nonchalantly in the opposite direction.

For a heart-stopping moment, I thought it might be Blondie or Buzzcut. My heart skipped a beat, icy fear coursing through my veins.

As I continued my walk, the thought of Zarek flickered through my mind. What if it was him? Had last night really been the last time he'd seen me? The idea lingered, both comforting and disconcerting, as I made my way through the dimly lit streets, feeling the weight of unseen eyes tracking my every step.

The moment I sank into the couch, my phone lit up with a call from my mom. I stared at the screen as it rang. I didn't have the energy to answer, but when she called a second time, a flicker of concern nudged my fatigue aside. She never called me twice in a row.

"Mom?" My voice cracked slightly as I finally answered. "Is everything okay?"

"Ora! Why aren't you picking up? I called you so many times!"

"You called once, Mom. I was just getting settled in. What's going on?" I tried to keep my tone light, brushing off the irritation.

She sighed. "Oh nothing. Just your father is annoying me. He wants us to take a trip to Hawaii. I told him I don't want to leave you by yourself."

"Mom, I already *am* by myself. I think it'd be nice if you go."

"Are you sure? After everything, I just…" Her voice trailed off, the unspoken fears hanging heavy between us. She was clearly alluding to that terrifying time two years ago when I had ended up in the hospital, after being brutally stabbed by my ex-boyfriend. It was only natural for my parents to worry.

"Yeah, Mom, I'm sure. It's been two years. I'm doing okay," I reassured her, even though part of me tightened at the reminder. "Really, go enjoy Hawaii. I'll be fine."

There was a pause, heavy with her lingering anxiety. "Okay, Ora, if you're sure. Just promise me you'll call if you need anything?"

"I promise, Mom." I smiled, though she couldn't see it. "Love you."

"Love you, too, honey. Did you hear about—"

"Mom," I cut her off. "I...can we chat later? I just—I'm not feeling too well."

"Oh, is everything okay? Is it your period?"

I rolled my eyes even though she couldn't see me. "No, Mom. Not my period. I'm just tired. I just got back from the gym and I don't have the energy left."

"Well, when *do* you?" she taunted.

"I'm sorry, Mom. Say hi to Dad for me, okay?"

There was a beat of silence on her end. And then she spoke again. "Ora. We worry, you know. You haven't been dating anyone and you're lonely, honey."

This again.

"God! I'm not lonely, Mom. I like living by myself. Honestly. Drop it. I know you think what happened still bothers me. It doesn't. I promise." I winced internally as the massive lies slipped out of me.

"Okay, honey. Just...take care of yourself, okay?"

"Yeah, Mom. I'll talk to you later, okay? Bye now."

As I hung up, the weight of their constant worry pressed down on me. Two years, and yet the shadow of the past still loomed large. I wanted to forget, but even more than that, I wished my friends and family could erase it from their memory too.

Since Adriano, I hadn't let anyone else in. The idea of being close to another man, potentially as cruel as he had been, made my skin crawl. I couldn't stomach the thought of surrendering control to someone else again. Adriano and I had been together for only seven months, but the final month was lost to me. The bits and pieces I did remember, only served as the testament to my naivety. How stupid I had been, to think love was supposed to feel like that.

Suddenly, the image of Zarek infiltrated my thoughts. A shiver ran down my spine, but not from fear. His sharply defined features—the angular face, the stern jawline—somehow brought a mix of intimidation and intrigue that I hadn't felt in a long time.

"So, he's dead, huh?" Ally's question jolted me back into our ongoing conversation about Adriano. There I was, sitting with her at this patio restaurant a few days later, my gaze darting around nervously, almost instinctively scanning for that untraceable watchfulness I felt.

"Yep, dead and gone. Guess that rules out worrying about his parole in seven years," I mumbled, poking at my eggs benedict without much appetite.

"Well, I'm just glad to have my friend back... Well, almost back. You seem a million miles away these days." Ally's voice was tinged with a mix of concern and curiosity.

I met her eyes briefly as she tilted her wine glass against the sunlight, casting a warm glow on her face.

"What do you mean? I'm right here, Allison."

That drew a small laugh from her. "Ooh, full name basis, huh? You know you only do that when you're on edge. What's up?"

I couldn't help but smile, albeit faintly. "It's just... something happened a few days ago. It's been stuck in my head."

Her expression shifted from playful to keen in an instant. "You met someone, didn't you?"

"Fuck no!" I blurted out, a bit too loudly.

Her grin widened, mischief twinkling in her eyes. "You did!" She pointed at me accusingly, her voice crescendoing to a dramatic wail. "And he's handsome, isn't he?"

I sighed, my slight twitch giving me away. "Ally, please, lower your voice. We're not alone here."

She leaned forward, her voice hushed but filled with excitement. "Spill it then. How did you meet Mr. Mystery?"

Wincing at the thought of explaining the potentially illegal circumstances of our meeting, I chose my words carefully. "Let's just say I helped him. And now, I think he might be watching over me. Might be him, you know?"

Her eyes widened in alarm. "Girl, no! You helped some random guy and now he's stalking you?"

If you think about it like that? Well...

Trying to brush off her concern—and my own—I managed a weak laugh. "Maybe I'm just being paranoid? It's nothing."

But Ally wasn't convinced and kept probing. "Describe him to me, then. What does he look like?"

Begrudgingly, I let slip about his striking appearance, maybe even mentioned something about a 'Greek god', which only fueled her curiosity.

As brunch stretched into late afternoon, we wrapped up, still chatting animatedly. Before parting ways, I half-jokingly, half-seriously made her promise not to mention my potential 'stalker' situation to my parents. "They're in Hawaii, Ally. They don't need this kind of stress."

She agreed, but I could tell her mind was racing with the romantic possibilities. Meanwhile, I couldn't shake the feeling of eyes on me as I walked away, the sensation oddly comforting yet unnerving.

FOUR

Leora

After another grueling day at work, my feet dragged me back to my apartment. Work had been brutal this past week, with back-to-back consultations and the relentless buzzing of my phone with notifications that I was too spent to check. I even skipped gym today, wanting to rest instead of spending an hour punching my dread away. But all that seemed like a reprieve compared to the scene that greeted me as I unlocked my door and pushed it open.

Panic gripped me. The place was trashed. My eyes darted around the disarray—the books tossed from their shelves, some lying face down, their spines cracked.

For one paralyzing moment, I was back in a darker time, the fear so tangible it was almost a physical presence in the room. My mind raced to the worst conclusion—Adriano. Could he have found a way back from the grave to torment me? The thought was irrational, yet fear isn't always ruled by logic. My breath hitched, and I stood frozen by the door, afraid of what more I might discover if I moved.

My heart sank further when I saw the shattered portrait of my cat, Ada. "Seriously?" I muttered, my voice shaking a bit with anger.

Kneeling to pick up the pieces, the harsh reality of someone breaking into my private life hit hard. "Fucking hell." I grumbled, trying to mask the hurt with annoyance as I cleaned up the mess.

The living room was a disaster, but I needed to check the rest of the apartment. My footsteps were hesitant as I pushed open my bedroom door. Everything seemed untouched here. I breathed a slight sigh of relief, though the comfort was superficial. The spare room and bathroom were the same—undisturbed, which somehow made the living room's chaos feel even more random.

I returned to the living room, trying to put some order back into it.

I picked up a fallen book, trying to restore some order to the chaos, when my phone suddenly buzzed to life. It caught me off guard—an unknown number flashing across the screen. My heart skipped a beat as I swiped to answer, my stomach in knots.

"Hello?" My voice came out stronger than I felt.

Only silence answered back. My pulse hammered in my ears. Could it be him? "Zarek?" I whispered into the void, half-hoping he would reveal himself.

Instead, a heavy sigh echoed through the line, followed by the sharp click of the call ending. "Coward," I muttered under my breath, my initial fear quickly burning up into frustration. This had to be connected to that night, to him— the night that sent my life spiraling out of control. Who else could it be, and why else would my apartment be turned upside down the moment things started getting weird?

Clutching my phone in my hand, I couldn't shake the feeling of eyes on me. My apartment no longer felt safe. I moved to the kitchen, my movements jittery. I grabbed a glass and filled it with water, my hands trembling slightly. Every sound seemed amplified, every shadow a hiding place.

My mind raced with possibilities—could it be Zarek? Why would he trash my place? Or was it someone else? Someone I pissed off at work, perhaps?

I slammed the water glass down harder than I meant to, the water spilling unceremoniously over the counter. I knew I had to tell someone about this, but what exactly? I rolled the idea around in my head, knowing too well how these stalking claims usually played out. "It's random," they'd dismiss, seeing nothing was stolen, just things tossed around. I muttered a curse under my breath, feeling the walls of my own home close in around me.

As night crept in, the isolation of the apartment grew heavier. I double-checked the locks on the doors and windows, my earlier defiance slowly dissolving into a gnawing anxiety. The locked door didn't stop them before. I truly wasn't safe.

The thought of sleep was laughable now. Instead, I settled onto the couch, a blanket pulled tight around me, waiting for the dawn or whatever might come first.

✧ ✧ ✧

"I swear, Mom, I really am driving. Like, right now," I said as I gripped the steering wheel tighter. A few sleepless nights had passed since my place was turned upside down, and I couldn't handle the eerie quiet of my apartment any longer. So, decision made, I was en route to my parents' place in Milton for some much-needed peace.

"How's the car holding up? You know how Ally is with maintenance," my mom's voice crackled through the speaker, tinged with concern. Originally, I had considered the train, avoiding the hassle of traffic. But the idea of being so exposed, surrounded by strangers' prying eyes, made my skin crawl. Borrowing Ally's somewhat neglected car seemed the lesser of two evils.

"It's holding up, Mom. It moves, and right now, that's enough," I reassured her, eyes flicking to the GPS. "I'll be there in about forty-three minutes." Traffic was a nightmare today, a relentless stream of cars, and I couldn't shake the feeling of being watched. *Again.* A particular car had been trailing me since I left my apartment, its persistence gnawing at my nerves.

On a sudden impulse, driven more by a need to confirm my fears than actual navigation, I swerved off at an exit way before my intended one. Glancing in the rearview mirror, my stomach sank as I saw the car blatantly follow my lead.

I rounded the corner and there it was again—a few cars back, subtle but unmistakable. For a fleeting moment, I entertained the thought that maybe, just maybe, they were after Ally.

Wishful thinking, Leora. They're tailing you.

Pushing that uneasy thought aside, I steered back

onto the highway, heading towards Milton. The mysterious car flickered in and out of view in my rearview mirror, keeping pace but never overtaking. It wasn't until I hit the quieter, tree-lined streets of the suburban neighborhood that the car finally vanished.

Shortly after, I pulled up to my parents' cozy little house in the heart of Milton. I scanned every shadow and corner as I got out of the car, half-expecting someone to leap out at any moment. My walk to the front door was a mix of casual strides and internal panic, my gut twisting with every step.

I didn't even pause to greet my mother when she opened the door, instead blurting out, "Hey, just need the bathroom!" as I dashed past her.

Once in the guest bathroom, I leaned against the door, trying to steady my breathing and calm the storm inside me.

After a few moments, I managed to pull myself together and strolled back into the living room as if nothing had happened, sinking into the couch next to my mom.

"Can I get a hug now?" she asked, her voice dry with mock irritation.

I let out a short laugh and wrapped her in a long, tight hug, still feeling the tremors of anxiety fading from my body. "Where's Dad?" I asked casually, letting my gaze wander around the room, still half-expecting trouble to follow me inside.

"He's in the backyard, covering the patio furniture. Can you believe we're expecting rain in March?" she said, but my mind wasn't ready to shift to mundane topics.

I simply nodded, a forced smile painting my face.

"There she is!" My dad announced his entrance,

rather dramatically.

"Hey, Dad!" I sprang up to hug him, instantly feeling the comforting, familiar safety of being near both him and Mom.

"What do you want to eat?" Mom peered at me with that scrutinizing look only mothers have. "You look thinner. Have you been eating properly? Hitting the gym?"

"Let the girl breathe, honey," Dad chimed in, giving me a supportive pat on the back.

"How was Hawaii?" I asked.

"Oh it was wonderful! It's such a beautiful place. You should go there sometime. Perfect for couples." My mom's slight nudge towards me finding someone, didn't go unnoticed. But I wasn't really in a mood to address it. We talked a bit more about their trip until a comfortable silence enveloped us.

Eventually, we gathered in the dining room where I could finally enjoy a real meal, something I hadn't prioritized lately. The first bite of the brisket melted in my mouth.

God, I missed this.

Sitting there, feeling a bit more grounded, I realized there was a difficult piece of news I hadn't yet shared. Clearing my throat abruptly, I plunged in without any buildup. "Adriano is dead."

Their heads comically whipped up. The shock on their faces told me they hadn't expected to hear his name tonight—or any night, really. After nearly two years of silence on that chapter of my life, this news was a jolt.

Mom clutched Dad's arm, her fingers trembling slightly.

"How?" Dad's voice was tight, his nostrils flaring.

"Some other inmate killed him," I said with a shrug that felt heavier than I intended.

"Are you okay, Ora?" Mom's voice quivered, the worry evident in her eyes.

I met their concerned looks with a forced smile. Adriano's death, while significant, didn't drag me back into the abyss as it once would have. Sure, the shadows of his terror lingered, but now, my mind was occupied with more immediate concerns, like a fucking stalker breaking into my apartment.

Oh, and let's not forget my road companion.

"I'm absolutely fine. It's a relief, really." My attempt at cheer sounded hollow even to my ears. "We don't have to worry about bumping into him ever again."

Dad cleared his throat, his expression skeptical. "Should we set up a session with Dr. Montez? You could do a session—"

"I'm fine, Dad," I cut him off, perhaps too sharply. "Really, I think this is the closure I needed."

Mom nodded, though her eyes mirrored the storm of doubt and relief warring within her. Dad, however, continued to scrutinize me, searching my face for something.

I understood pretty quickly why he eyed me like that. His next words sent an alarm ringing through my body, "Ora, honey... did you—were you in any way involved?"

"Oliver!" Mom's hand landed a sharp smack on his thigh, a clear rebuke.

"I'm just asking! That man was the devil. He nearly killed our daughter," Dad countered.

"Dad, no, I had nothing to do with it. Sure, I've fantasized about it, but you know me—I wouldn't actually do something like that." I raised my hands in a gesture of innocence.

"Good," he sighed and gave me a small smile. "But we would've sided with you, anyway."

It was bizarre, hearing my parents indirectly condone murder, even if it was just theoretical support.

"I wouldn't expect anything else." I smiled back.

Dinner wrapped up quicker than usual, and it was time for me to head back. I'd been picking up extra shifts at work, using the long hours as an excuse to stay away from my apartment. Ever since that break-in, I'd been on edge—half expecting to come home to another intrusion or worse, someone lurking in the shadows waiting for me.

During the drive back home, my mind replayed every detail of my visit with my parents, distracting me from the nagging anxiety. It wasn't until the familiar headlights appeared in my rearview mirror that I snapped back to reality. The same car that had followed me in the morning was tailing me again. Oddly enough, this time it didn't stir panic within me.

As I parked near my building, the car vanished as if it had never been there. I'd caught brief glimpses of the driver a few times—close enough to make out features that were unsettlingly familiar. Was it Zarek? Why would he be following me so openly? Shaking my head, I tried to brush off the creeping suspicion as I fumbled with my keys.

Stepping into my apartment, I half-expected chaos—more signs of intrusion. But what greeted me was utter, dreadful silence.

FIVE

Zarek

I'd always kept to a strict rule: keep everyone at arm's length. My squad was my family, and my real family had no part in this life I lived. It worked well, until it didn't.

That night changed everything. I'd been ambushed, down but not out, ready to fight back. That's when she appeared, throwing punches and kicks with a wild ferocity that stunned me into stillness. I watched, dumbfounded, my ass planting itself firmly to the ground. Later, I found myself inviting myself to her apartment, not wanting the night to end so unceremoniously.

Now, here I was, lurking in the shadows of her apartment building after ensuring she returned safely from her trip to Milton. I had made certain no threats lingered this time. The memory of seeing Calzone Romano, that thug from that chaotic night, lurking near her place still sent a shiver of anger through me.

When he had dared to climb her apartment stairs,

instinct overrode everything else. But dealing with him—well, it was simpler to leave her with a trashed apartment than to leave her with a body to explain.

She was safely inside her apartment, now. I lingered a moment longer, watching the flicker of lights as she moved through her rooms, making sure everything was as usual before heading back to my car. Then I drove back to the headquarters, my thoughts whirring.

Initially, I maintained enough distance to ensure she remained unaware, to keep the illusion that she wasn't being watched. But the restraint that came so naturally in my line of work began to crumble under her inadvertent pull. It wasn't just watching anymore; it felt like she was reaching into the very depths of me, clawing at my control.

One slip—she caught a glimpse of me—and my carefully laid plans to remain hidden disintegrated. I found myself following her more openly, driven by a compulsion I couldn't tamp down. Every time I saw her scan her surroundings, the rapid beat of her pulse visible at her throat, or the subtle tremor in her hands as she clutched her bag a little tighter, my heart thundered with a mix of dread and thrill. It was as if she could feel my presence, feel the intensity of my gaze. Feel *me*.

I knew I had to pull back, to return to the shadows where I belonged. I had already eliminated Calzone, and his brother, Casteel, was next. Once he was dealt with, I promised myself I would step back, that I'd let her go on with her life relatively untouched.

Yet, the thought of cutting ties left a hollow ache in my chest. Ending this mission meant losing this unintended connection with her, a connection that somehow felt like the most real thing in my world.

I slammed the door of my car and strode past Logan and Dylan without a word, all the way to my room. I booted up my laptop in a hurry. There she was on the screen, clutching the blanket tighter than she had the day before, perched on the armchair instead of the couch. The urge to hear her voice surged, tempting me to dial her number again, but I slammed the laptop shut as the thought crossed my mind.

You've got to stop this, Zar.

Descending the stairs, I noticed Logan and Dylan had vanished. Relief washed over me—I wasn't ready to face them, not with this secret eating at me. They'd see right through me, maybe even try to knock some sense into me.

In the corridor, I caught Kabir's eye and jerked my head toward the gym. "Any news on Casteel Romano?" I pressed as soon as the gym door clicked shut behind us.

Kabir shot me a look, the kind that said he knew I was off balance. "Boss, this has to stop. I'm running out of excuses for the squad around your disappearance."

"Casteel," I snapped, cutting him off. "Any news on him?"

"Nothing," he sighed, running a hand through his hair. "He's covering his tracks. Unlike Calzone, who went straight for your girl—predictable. But Casteel's being careful."

My mind raced with the implications. "And Calzone? The body?"

"Disposed of," he confirmed grimly.

Kabir's face tightened with concern. "Look,

Ghost, everyone knows I'm chasing Casteel for you. And with all your 'stakeouts,' they're going to connect the dots. You need to shut it down or get her some protection. Sebastian can—"

"I know." I said. "I know, Kabir. I never meant for her to get dragged into this mess. It's on me. She's in danger because of what I did. I fucking *know*!"

He hesitated, then added, "You broke protocol the night you went to her place. You made her a target by linking her to us. I'm not saying it's your fault but…"

"It's my fault," I admitted, the guilt heavy in my voice. A simple misstep, and now she was in the crosshairs. I was driven by something deeper than duty now, something perilously close to obsession, and it was putting her at risk.

Fuck.

"Just get Casteel for me. Put your tech skills to work!" I gritted out and left without giving him a chance to respond.

✧ ✧ ✧

Staring at the screen, watching a woman scared shitless in the confines of her own home, is a turn I didn't think my life would take. How were her movements jittery yet still graceful?

She, indeed, was my warrior goddess, fighting this new unseen enemy with whatever she could.

Her eyes, wide and flickering with both fear and a spark that might have been determination, scanned the room. It was clear she was a walking paradox; courageous yet visibly shaken.

"I know you're watching me!" she yelled, her words echoing off the walls. I froze, the cold fear that she might have discovered the cameras settling in. Had she seen the one hidden in the living room? Or on the balcony? *God*, the bedroom too…

She hardly ever slept in her bedroom anymore, always on edge, always ready. I found myself wondering how she managed any rest on that cramped couch.

Her voice broke through my thoughts again, stronger this time but quivering with an undercurrent of fear. "I don't know how, but I know I'm being watched. If it's you, and you know who you are, fucking face me, coward!"

The blend of anger and vulnerability in her tone did something to me. Her trembling yet fierce defiance made my heart race, and I felt myself harden at the thought of her actually finding me in her apartment. Hell, I *wanted* to be there.

I slammed my laptop shut, a harsh clack echoing around the room, and let out a ragged sigh. I needed a cold shower—like I had been, every fucking day.

SIX

Leora

More days slipped by, and the details of Zarek's visit began to blur, which unsettled me more than I cared to admit. I found myself clinging to the remnants of his memory—his resonant voice and the sculpted lines of his powerful body.

Stop it. He's probably your stalker.

As my birthday weekend approached, I wasn't exactly thrilled about celebrating. But a handful of my closest friends, including the irrepressible Ally, had other ideas. They orchestrated a small house party at my place, and despite my protests, I found myself swept up in their plans.

Ally bounced on the couch as she laid out her idea. "Let's hit a club!" she proposed, her eyes sparkling with the thought of neon lights and dance floors.

"Sure." I sarcastically laughed it off.

"Perfect!" Ally clapped her hands, a grin spreading

across her face.

Ah, fuck.

Just then, Jenna walked in, carrying bags of chips and a suspiciously wobbly cake that looked like it had seen better days.

"Are we really doing this? Going clubbing?" Max asked, eyebrows raised as he helped Jenna set down the snacks on the coffee table.

Jenna chimed in with a smirk. "Why not, Max? It's not like we have anything better to do at one in the morning. We'll eat the cake after, I promise."

Glancing at the clock, I noticed it was already 1:35 AM. "Isn't it a bit late for clubbing?" I asked, half-hoping they'd take the hint and settle for a quiet night in.

"Hey, no worries—there are a few clubs that don't close until 3 AM," Ally reassured everyone, waving off my concerns with a dismissive hand.

"Let me rephrase," I corrected, "Isn't it too old for us to be hitting a club?"

"Speak for yourself!" Ally rolled her eyes grinning. She was the youngest of us all.

Max plopped down next to Jenna, his hand caressing her thigh. "Which clubs are these? And more importantly, do they serve decent drinks, or are we talking about beer that tastes like it's been brewed in a bathtub?"

Jenna punched Max lightly on the arm. "Come on, it'll be fun. And besides, it's Leora's birthday. We can't let her spend it just lounging around here, can we?"

"Fine, let's do this," I declared, begrudgingly. "But if we end up at a club with bathtub beer, Ally is buying the first round."

"Deal!" Ally agreed, raising her hands in mock

surrender.

With that settled, we gathered our things.

Thirty minutes later, we spilled into Century, a club pulsing with the kind of energy that could erase all your worries—or at least drown them out for a while. I had slipped into a chic, short dress that felt daringly out of character for me. I shucked off my coat at the door, hoping my ever-present shadow had taken the night off. Tonight, I didn't feel the usual prickle of being watched.

Inside, the club was a riot of lights and sound, each beat of the music thumping against my chest like a second heartbeat. We carved out a little island for ourselves on the dance floor, letting loose among a sea of bodies. Jenna and Max, the newest couple in our crew, were practically glued together, lost in their new love bubble. They just couldn't keep their mouths from each other.

As the thudding music pulsed in time with my heartbeat, a strange unease crept over me. It was as if my body was rejecting the distraction, craving the silence instead. So after a few songs, I excused myself and headed out.

Standing alone outside the club around 2:30 AM, I lit a cigarette, the streets quieting as the night drew to a close. The crisp night air felt good against my skin, a welcome reprieve from the pulsing music.

Suddenly, I felt a looming presence behind me. My skin prickled, mingling with dread that had my stomach tied in knots. My shadow was never this close. *Never.*

And this presence was anything but protective. It felt ominous.

"Finally out of the cage, little bird," a voice hissed

from the darkness behind me. Suddenly, I wished I hadn't been skipping gym for the past few days.

The next second, my world flipped. A rough hand clamped down on my shoulder, spinning me around. The sudden movement jolted me, my cigarette tumbling to the ground. The bright ember fizzled out as it hit the pavement.

I angled myself to drop a sharp elbow to his face, but then I felt it—a sharp prick on the side of my neck. Cold dread washed over me as the realization hit: I was being drugged. The world began to tilt, sounds and lights blurring into a disorienting cacophony. My limbs grew heavier, my thoughts muddled and slow, stealing my ability to fight, to scream.

"My girlfriend's just drunk, man," said the same muffled voice, trying to sound casual as he dragged me away. Panic surged through me; my limbs locked up, completely unresponsive despite my desperate attempts to break free. An overwhelming fear enveloped me, more intense and terrifying than anything I'd ever known.

I squinted through the heavy haze clouding my vision, my eyes straining for a sliver of clarity. There—he was a silhouette from a nightmare, the one I called Blondie, his identity clicking into place even as my capacity to react slipped away.

My world narrowed down to a pinprick of awareness, then blinked out entirely.

✧ ✧ ✧

As my eyes adjusted to the darkness of the room, a fog of grogginess enveloped my senses. Abruptly, a sharp slap cut through the silence, jolting me into painful awareness. It wasn't the first; my cheeks throbbed with the sting of multiple hits, each one, brutal.

"What the fuck do you want, Blondie?" I growled through the pain, my voice hoarse and strained.

"Blondie?" he laughed, a cold, mocking sound that chilled the air. "Name's Casteel, little bird. Now tell me where Grant is. The guy you were with that night?"

Grant.

"I don't know him. He ran off shortly after you pussies did," I managed to spit out, my throat searing as if scorched by acid, suggesting I might have been choked earlier.

Sadistic bastards.

"Fuck. I think this bitch was just in the wrong place, wrong time," someone murmured to Casteel in the background.

Ignoring the comment, Casteel leaned closer, his breath foul against my face. "Listen," he hissed, "he killed my brother. So you better tell me where he is or I'll display your fucking body on a crosswalk."

A bitter laugh escaped me despite the danger. "He doesn't care. He doesn't even know me, you idiots."

Deep down, I prayed that my shadow was Zarek. That he'd somehow come for me.

"Fine, just keep her alive," Casteel finally conceded. Then he whispered with a smirk. "For now."

"Can I play with her a little?" The other guy. His insinuation stirred a different kind of panic within me.

Before I could retaliate, the room tilted slightly as I tried to find a sliver of strength, but the darkness began to creep in again at the edges of my vision. A sharp slap rang in my ears and my body succumbed once more to unconsciousness.

SEVEN

Zarek

"So this is what you've been doing, huh?" Logan's voice hit me like a cold splash, jolting me from my stakeout haze.

"What are you doing here, Gunner?" I rolled my eyes, irritated that I'd been caught.

"What, just enjoying the show, watching you gawk at her, *Ghost!*" He chuckled.

"I'm not gawking. She got mixed up in something that night. I just want to make sure she doesn't end up in trouble," I defended sternly, my gaze locked on Leora's lively figure among the throng of club-goers celebrating her birthday.

"Well, nothing's happened. As you can clearly see," Logan retorted. Only if he knew what Calzone had done, breaking into her apartment.

"And nothing will." I replied firmly. "I can't have civilians caught in the crossfire because of our mistakes,"

"*Your* mistake, Zarek. You let her step into this

mess." Logan said pointedly.

I shook my head, a mix of anger and guilt swirling inside me. I wanted to argue, to defend my actions, but the lump in my throat held back any plausible denials. He was right, and we both knew it.

Turning to face him, I admitted. "So, Kabir told you."

He shook his head. "I figured it out myself. You've been focused on Casteel so much that you've forgotten what this mission is about. All I had to do was wait for Kabir to slip up a bit. Which was easier than I thought."

I bowed my head in defeat. "I can't not watch over her, Logan."

"And that includes putting cameras in her apartment. I see." He said blankly.

"How the fuck—you know what, fuck it. That night messed everything up."

"Nope. *You* did. I told you to call for backup that night," Logan reminded me. "But you just *had* to do surveillance by yourself."

"I didn't expect there to be two perps. I was just following one lead." I said curtly.

He chuckled. "And that gave you a gash on your stomach with a side of obsession."

My gut churned at the word. I *was* obsessed.

"Great, now she's going inside in that stupid dress," Logan pointed at Leora and her friends showing their IDs to the bouncer outside. "Are we waiting until she's out?"

She was laughing now, surrounded by friends in a bubble of joy that seemed a world away from me.

Let her be, Zar. At least for tonight.

"No, *we* are leaving," I said reluctantly.

I nudged Logan back toward his car parked across from Club Century and climbed in. As Logan drove off, the city lights blurred past, mirroring the turmoil in my mind. Thirty minutes later, we arrived at Alpha Squad Six's headquarters.

My decoy phone rang as I got out of the car. This was the number I gave to civilians or police officers to get in touch with me. I eyed the unknown number, fear washing over me. The last person I gave this number to was the bouncer at the club. Walking inside I answered the call.

"It's Chase. You gave me your number to report anything unusual?" His calm voice sounded. For a brief moment I felt relieved. He was calm. How bad could it be?

"Yes. What have you got?" I said, my voice mirroring his calm.

"The girl you described... well, she was really drunk just now. Her boyfriend was dragging her into a car. Not sure if this counts as—"

I hung up, my heart stopped for a terrifying moment. In an instant, I was back in action, sprinting back to the car.

Logan was right behind me. "Talk to me, Ghost."

"She was taken. Someone snatched her off the fucking street." I muttered as I quickly geared up and jumped into the driver's seat. Logan soundlessly followed me.

Peeling off our street, I barked into the phone, calling Kabir, "I need your eyes on a vehicle. Logan will give you the approximate location."

After passing the phone to Logan, I raced back towards the club, desperate hope fueling my drive that it wasn't Leora who had been taken. Upon arriving, I zeroed in on a convenience store across the street.

Barging into the store, I made a beeline for the cashier who was mundanely stacking shelves. "I need to see your security tapes facing the street. *Now!*" My voice was more of a command than a request.

The cashier, a young guy with a bewildered look, started to stammer a response. I didn't have time for hesitation. I flashed my decoy police badge I kept for occasions just like this. "Official business. I need to see the footage from forty minutes ago."

As he scrambled to comply, I couldn't keep still. My leg tapped an urgent rhythm on the linoleum floor.

"Relax," Logan tried to reassure me, his voice steady. "We'll get her back safely."

I rounded on him, my fear spilling over into anger. "You're assuming it was her that was taken!" I bellowed, the possibility gnawing at my insides.

"But you said—" Logan raised his hands as his eyes met my icy glare. "You know what, screw it. All I'm saying is, *if* it's her, we're going to find her. Trust me. Kabir's already on it."

I redirected my focus just as the store employee managed to pull up the desired footage. My breath hitched, my heart thudding ominously as the grainy images flickered to life on the screen.

"Fuck!" The curse slipped out as my worst fears materialized before my eyes. There she was—Leora, unmistakable even in the poor quality video, her body limp in the grasp of a familiar brute. She looked helpless and I felt bile rise up my throat.

Logan leaned closer, his eyes narrowing as he recognized the assailant. "That's Casteel Romano."

"I know." I snarled. "Does Kabir have a location

yet?"

Logan's phone buzzed at that exact moment, and he glanced at it, a crooked grin spreading across his face as he read the message. "Got something. He's traced her to an old apartment on the northeast side."

The surge of energy that shot through me was palpable, a fierce cocktail of fear and determination. "Let's go!" I barked, already heading for the door.

✧ ✧ ✧

The apartment building stood isolated on the outskirts of the Greater Toronto Area, its once vibrant paint now peeling away in ragged strips, revealing the weary bones of a structure long neglected.

"Third floor, south-facing apartment. Belongs to Casteel's girlfriend," Logan whispered, his voice low under the cloak of night. I gave him a curt nod, feeling the weight of the moment tighten around my chest as I made my way to the fire escape, the metal cold and unyielding under my hands. Logan opted for the main entrance, planning to blend in just another day's end.

I ascended with cautious agility, reaching the third floor to find myself facing a row of windows, some cracked, others fogged. Peering into what looked like an empty room, I muttered a curse under my breath. She wasn't here—or perhaps not in this apartment at all.

Climbing through the window, I was greeted by the room's stale air, thick with the scent of neglect. Almost immediately, I heard Casteel's distinct voice from the living room, his tone laced with frustration.

"No, she's saying she doesn't know him. This whole thing was stupid. He would've shown up by now. Why do you think I didn't switch cars?"

Stealthily, I moved toward the room's exit, my gun raised and ready. As I stepped through the doorway, Casteel's head snapped up, and his lips twisted into a smile—a chilling, unsettling smile.

"I got him," he said into the phone with eerie calmness before hanging up and raising his hands in surrender.

"Where is she?" The words scraped from my throat, hoarse and strained.

"Oh, the little bird?" He was grinning now. "She'll be fine. Unless you try to do something stupid." He strolled aimlessly across the living room. "You know, like, kill me?"

I moved slightly closer to him. I needed him alive, but that didn't mean his kneecaps needed to stay intact.

He continued, "You pull that trigger, Grant. And see how beautiful she'd look with a hole in her head."

My breath came in short sprints. I needed to stay calm.

Where the fuck is Logan?

I edged him towards one of the rooms and he confidently followed my lead.

"I'll take great pleasure in killing you, Casteel. Just like I did with Calzone." I declared.

His grin fell, morphing into a scowl. "You'll pay for what you did."

I nudged him further into the room. My finger itching to pull that trigger. But I knew I couldn't. Leora could be killed.

Before I could lunge at him, something flew right

by my ear, lodging into Casteel's shoulder. A knife. I peered back to see Logan shrugging.

"You fucking—"

Before Casteel could finish his sentence, I acted, my emotions boiling over. I shut him inside the room he was caged in. His muffled scream sliced through the tension and I panicked. This could alert someone to take the shot at Leora.

I ran to the only other room in the apartment, leaving Logan to deal with Casteel.

My heart pounded with dread as I pushed open the door. I braced myself for what might come next. But nothing could have prepared me for the sight that greeted me in that room—a sight that sent a shockwave of anger through me.

Leora was tied up in a chair and unconscious while this other man held her head up to line her mouth with his dick. My eyes hazed for a moment, unable to register what was happening in front of me. The man's head snapped in my direction and I didn't think, I just shot. It went right through his length as he fell to the floor writhing in pain. His guttural screams echoing off the walls.

I dashed to Leora, quickly untying her and pulling her into my arms. Her body was limp, and a wave of panic surged through me as I whispered urgently into her ear, "Leora?"

She didn't stir for a moment and my finger flew to her neck to feel a pulse.

"Wake up, Leora. *Fuck!*" I was losing it.

The thudding of her heartbeat under my fingers was the only solace in the room. She murmured faintly, her words lost beneath the incessant screaming from the asshole, grating on my nerves.

Fucking hell. With an exasperated sigh, I yanked my gun up and emptied a bullet into his head.

Now, I can hear her better.

She stirred again, mumbled something incoherent and my head dropped to hers with relief.

"Zarek?" her voice was faint, almost lost.

"Yes, I'm here. Fuck, this should never have happened." Gently, I brushed tangled strands of hair from her face.

"I guess we're even, now," she murmured with a mix of breathlessness and roughness in her voice.

"Let's get you out of here, okay?"

Carefully, I lifted her into my arms, carrying her away from the dark confines of that apartment and into the safety of my car parked outside.

"Casteel bolted through the fire escape." Logan said, slightly irritated with himself. "I didn't want to leave you guys here."

I nodded. My focus shifted to the girl in my arms, her faint breaths warm on my neck.

"Find him." I instructed.

"Yeah, I'll try to find the asshole. You take the car," Logan sighed, tossing the keys to me.

As we made our way to the headquarters, Leora's awareness seemed to sharpen. She gazed out the window, her expression unreadable, her silence unnerving.

"Can you walk?" I asked, my voice tight with worry as I supported her out of the car. My heart was still pounding fiercely, haunted by how close we'd come to something unimaginably horrifying.

"Yeah, I can walk," she said tersely, shrugging off my hand and moving steadily toward the three-story house we stood before in the driveway.

"Are you feeling okay?" I ventured, catching up to her as I opened the gate with a keycode and my thumbprint.

She walked through without a word, her silence heavy between us. Inside, she paused and turned to face me, her eyes somber, almost resigned.

"I need a bed to rest in," she said simply, her voice devoid of any warmth.

I led her to my upstairs room, offering her one of my T-shirts and a towel before excusing myself. As I closed the door behind me, her silence echoed louder than any words. She hadn't spoken anything meaningful since we left that horrific apartment, and the air between us felt charged with an unspoken reproach. I was left to wonder if she resented me, not just for the danger I'd exposed her to, but for the entire clusterfuck since we met.

EIGHT

Leora

I changed into the T-shirt Zarek/Grant gave me, which was barely longer than the dress I had been wearing. In the bathroom, I ran the towel under some hot water and began cleaning myself up as thoroughly as I could.

As I wiped away the remnants of the night, the sight of dark bruises blossoming across my legs, ribs, shoulders, and neck stopped me cold. Each mark felt like a betrayal of my body's boundaries, a painful reminder not just of last night, but of a past I'd struggled to move beyond. I stripped away my smeared makeup and washed my face, the water mixing with a bitter sting of memories from my time with Adriano—times when bruises had been more common than I cared to admit. I was angry. Frustrated that I'd let myself into yet another situation that made me lose control of my life.

Climbing into the warm sheets, sleep quickly overtook me despite the aching of my battered body.

When I awoke, the sunlight piercing through the window felt harsh, as though no time had passed at all.

I wondered what this place was. Zarek/Grant didn't seem like a police officer at all.

What have I gotten myself into?

The door creaked open and Zarek/Grant stepped in, carrying a tray of scrambled eggs, bacon, and juice. He placed it on the nightstand before sitting down at the foot of the bed. My gaze must have carried the weight of my unrest because his expression shifted to one of concern, his brows knitting together in worry.

"I am so sorry for what happened," he murmured sincerely.

"I got myself involved that night. It's not your fault, *Grant*," I said, though confusion clouded my mind about his true identity.

"It's Zarek," he clarified softly, as if he could read the confusion etched across my face. "My name is Zarek Rivera. Born in January, I am 35 years old."

"Hmm. Leora Mateez. March. I turned 29 yesterday," I replied.

"I know. Happy birthday," he said solemnly, his gaze dropping to the bruises on my neck. I instinctively covered them with my hand.

His Adam's apple bobbed as he swallowed hard, his discomfort palpable. "Eat and then meet me downstairs, okay?" He said, rising from the bed. He paused at the doorway, giving me one last look that carried some regret before he left the room.

After finishing the eggs and bacon, I took the glass of juice and headed downstairs. Suddenly conscious of the scant length of Zarek's T-shirt, I tugged at the hem, trying to cover more of myself, a small gesture of reclaiming some dignity after feeling so exposed.

Once downstairs, I noticed a man with dirty blond hair seated at the dining table, leisurely sipping from a cup while scrolling through his phone.

Zarek approached with a cup of his own and nodded towards the man as I followed his gaze.

"That's Logan," he introduced, just as Logan shot a glare at both of us.

Logan exhaled sharply, his frustration evident as he tossed his head back and groaned, "Fucking hell."

"What's wrong with him?" I inquired, a hint of annoyance threading through my curiosity.

"He's just pissed that I blew his cover," Zarek explained with a slight shrug.

"Then maybe you shouldn't be doing that. What if I'm a spy?" I countered, half-joking but also genuinely concerned about the casual reveal of sensitive information.

"See? At least she has some brains," Logan barked from across the room. He then turned to me, his tone dripping with sarcasm, "Hi Leora, lovely meeting you yesterday. Perhaps you should slip back into that skimpy dress you came in and walk on back to your place." Then he looked at Zarek. "This is no place for *civilians*."

His words, sharp and unwelcoming, stung more than I expected. "I don't intend to stay," I retorted sharply, my voice cold. I downed my glass of juice in one long gulp, handed the empty glass to Zarek with a forceful push against his chest, and turned to head back upstairs.

Their message was clear, I wasn't welcome here.

NINE

Zarek

"Are you fucking insane?" I bellowed at Logan as I quickly followed Leora to my bedroom, anger coursing through me.

The moment I entered, I realized my grave mistake—I hadn't knocked. Leora had taken off the T-shirt I had given her, her bare back exposed to me, clad only in her black panties as she turned her dress inside out. Hastily, I shut the door behind me to prevent anyone else from walking in on this private moment.

She glanced over her shoulder, a shudder rippling through her. "I guess it's your turn to watch me change and then get the fuck out of your space," she said, her voice laced with icy detachment.

"You're not leaving. It's not safe," I insisted, my concern peaking.

"Didn't you already neutralize the threat? Isn't that guy in your custody?" she huffed, frustration evident in her tone.

I sighed deeply, the weight of the situation pressing down on me. "No. He ran away. And he has more people on your tail. On *my tail*, fuck. Just… stay. Please, Leora."

Then, in a move that completely shattered my defenses, she turned around, exposing her breasts to me. I struggled to maintain eye contact, but my gaze involuntarily dropped, despite my best efforts. I swallowed as I studied the soft curves of her ample breasts, the tempting brown peeks desperate for my mouth. A small, knowing smile played on her lips.

"Like what you see?" She whispered softly.

A ragged breath escaped me as I felt my cock harden under my sweatpants.

God, these sweatpants won't stop from tenting.

As I approached her, my eyes involuntarily drifted to the bruise on her neck—a vivid reminder of yesterday's fuck up. A surge of fury washed over me again, momentarily overshadowing the fact that she was half-naked in my bedroom, on the verge of leaving.

Gently, I brushed the back of my hand against her throat, tracing the line down to the bruise on her shoulder. Leaning in close, my jaw brushed her arm as I picked up my T-shirt from the bed and draped it over her, covering her. Her eyes held mine in a steady gaze, and when she finally closed them as the fabric settled over her skin, I nearly lost it.

Thoughts of pressing my lips to hers left me momentarily dizzy with longing.

"You're not going anywhere, Leora. Not until this case is wrapped up," I said, my voice tight with an effort to keep steady.

"And what about my work? I have a job, you

know?"

I nodded. "For now, you need to stay hidden. They were probably following you this whole time."

"And what about you? Have you been following me these past few weeks, too?" Her question was direct.

"Yes," I admitted, feeling the weight of the confession.

She just nodded, her expression unreadable.

I rushed to justify my actions, "I needed to ensure—"

"Did you trash my apartment, too?"

I slowly shook my head, averting her icy gaze. "No. That was Calzone. One of the guys from that night."

"And the car, tailing me?"

"That was me." I said. "Leora. You need to understand—"

She raised her hand, silencing me. "I need to know what all you did. Were you following me prior to that night?"

"No. That was the first time I met you." Then I corrected myself. "Saw you."

"And after that?"

I took a deep breath, ready to take the plunge. "After that night, I followed you around work and tailed you during your commute. Then I saw Calzone entering your apartment and we had a…disagreement at your place. I'm sorry for the mess, by the way."

"Continue." She said blankly.

I cleared my throat off the lump that was lodged there. I knew my next words would make her hate me. Well, more than she already did. "I installed a camera in your living room." I heard her gasp, but I forced myself to continue. "And your balcony. And your bedroom."

She was shaking with anger, now. Her nostrils flared. "So, you saw me. Heard me calling you a fucking coward, which you are, by the way."

I closed my eyes and nodded, cursing myself for admitting that I'd been watching her.

Fuck. *Stalking* her.

"Why? You said you weren't flirting. So, why did you go to all these lengths? In the name of protection?"

"It started out that way." I said, the guilt becoming unbearable. "But I wanted to see you more. Protect you. Because it was my fault you were in this mess."

Her nod was contemplative. She studied my face for a bit and then, out of nowhere, threw me a curveball. "Do you have 14oz boxing gloves?"

Her question was so unexpected it momentarily wiped the guilt from my face.

"I'm sorry?" I blinked, confused.

"Boxing gloves. I want to punch this anger away. Or would you rather me punch your face right now?" she hissed.

I hesitated. "I–uh–only have the regular 16oz. Are you sure you're okay, though? Yesterday was—"

"That Logan guy can spar with me," she said curtly, ignoring my concerns.

"I can spar with you, too?" I asked gently, knowing I'd be shut down.

"No. I'd rather spar with someone who isn't a coward."

I managed a nod.

"Just tell him to keep his thoughts to himself," she added sharply.

I nodded again, still confused at her random request and left her in the room. Once downstairs, I sought out Amelia for some gym clothes. She handed them over with a knowing smirk.

Returning to my room, I found Leora had put the T-shirt back on and was waiting.

"Here," I handed her the clothes. "These are Amelia's."

"Is that her alias?"

"No. It's her real name... I think. Maybe she lied to us, who knows," I said with a light smile.

"What is this place? You're clearly not a cop," she asked, pulling the T-shirt over her head to change into the gym clothes. I turned around, playing the role of a gentleman, giving her privacy.

"It's a safe house and the headquarters of an intelligence division of law enforcement." I told her half the truth.

"So, you're like the FBI?"

"Sort of."

"And is stalking civilians part of your job description?"

"Only the ones that are in danger." I replied, turning back to face her just as she finished slipping into the shorts. "And don't ever show that body to anyone else like you did with me."

"Why?" she said defiantly.

My gaze hardened, unable to tear away from her, "Because not everyone will be as unaffected by it."

"So you were unaffected by it?"

"I'm trained not to get distracted by mere breasts, Leora."

Her face fell but kept her chin up.

"Understood. Now, tell your little Logan to bring

his best in the ring," she challenged, her tone light yet determined.

I forced a smile, "There's no ring. It's just a matted gym."

She nodded, then headed to the door, poised and ready, leaving me to stew in my stupidity.

✧ ✧ ✧

Thirty minutes later, I entered the gym to find Logan and Leora sparring. Logan was clearly holding back, his punches pulled and combinations far from lethal. Leora, on the other hand, displayed competent skills, though her punches seemed more like extensions of her arms rather than powerful blows originating from her core. When she attempted a body kick, I noticed the lack of protection on her shins. Grabbing the smallest shin guards that Amelia used, I walked over to intervene.

"Here. You need these before you injure yourself," I handed them over.

"Thanks," Leora said, panting.

I nodded at them to continue and walked back to a buzzing phone.

"Rivera 32577," I answered with my squad code.

"Brewer 28190, I have intel on Casteel. He was in contact with his cousin, Jerome Tyson. Son of Garret Tyson."

"Fuck," I muttered, frustration boiling inside me. Garret Tyson was a thorn in our side, deeply entrenched with the US and Chinese governments, facilitating critical trade routes for electronic goods and services. Rumors had even linked him to the 2024 US Presidential candidate George Aiden and the

Chinese President Xi Xiaxu. Our mission in Alpha Squad Six was to disrupt these trade routes without touching his other operations. *For now.*

Out of the nine original Bridgewood Alpha Squads, only three were operational and two were active, Squad Six, my crew, and Squad Two, Lancaster Brewer's crew.

"Copy. What's the current status of Jerome and Garret?"

Brewer continued. "Alive. The hideout is in Bali, Indonesia. They're keeping ops open using Casteel. You won't believe what they're trading now. Twenty-five units of Crazon were imported last Friday that you tried to intercept. It's an AI-based pocket watch. Does anything you would expect of a fucking high-end security unit."

"Is it available for sale? I'm assuming no, but need to confirm," I asked.

"Affirmative. Not for sale," after a moment's silence Lancaster cursed, "Fuck. There's another shipment approved by Candor Imports Inc. in Florida. It's owned by Jerome Tyson."

"Brewer, I need your squad in Florida. What's the destination?"

"You're not going to like this. It's Toronto. I think you should keep HQ safe. Move to a different safe house."

"Copy. I'll send you our new links in 48 hours. Goodbye."

I hung up and lowered my head at the gym table. Logan walked up behind me.

"Any developments?"

"Casteel is Jerome Tyson's cousin. Trading in new units of Crazon through Candor Imports in Florida.

Squad Two to intercept. We're on delivery as backup. We gotta move to a secondary location. Get the crew ready."

"What about her?" Logan jerked his chin up at Leora.

Fuck. Leaving her behind could make her a target again for Jerome and Casteel, who would use her to draw us out.

"She comes with us." I decided. She needed to be close, where I could ensure her safety.

Leaving Logan to relay the plan to Leora, I made a beeline for my room. I packed with military precision, stuffing essentials into a duffel bag. Every second counted.

As I thundered down the stairs, ready to swap the plates on our long-commuter SUVs, Amelia intercepted me. Her presence was a calm amidst the storm.

"Dylan and Kabir are ready to leave," she reported crisply.

"Great. Leave emergency ammo in the X6 and get the Escalade ready for me, Logan, and Leora. Can Leora borrow your clothes?" I asked, running a hand through my hair.

"I got Kabir to pick up some essentials from her apartment this afternoon," Amelia responded efficiently, her tone light but her eyes sharp with focus.

I nodded appreciatively. "This is why you're my best member."

Amelia's lips twitched. "Can I tell that to Logan?"

"Tell him after we're out of this mess," I quipped back, the corner of my mouth lifting in a rare smile despite the tension.

TEN

Leora

So, he'd been watching me. Actually stalking me. And he'd admitted it. But why did it bother me more that he was a coward, hiding in the shadows, rather than the fact that he was a stalker? Why did it irk me that he couldn't just protect me openly, instead of taking these sneaky, invasive steps? And dammit, why was I still caught up on the striking lines of his jaw? The irresistible ridges of his muscles?

Shit. Stop.

Every time I saw him, it was like a rush of all those intense, unfiltered desires came flooding back. I'd built up this image of him in my head, and somehow, he was still outdoing it.

'I'm trained to not get distracted by mere breasts, Leora.'

God! I wasn't sure why, but in that moment, compelled by a mix of defiance and a desire to test him, I had turned around and done something I hadn't had the courage to do in front of anyone for years. I just needed to see his reaction.

I exhaled a heavy sigh and shuffled outside to meet the team for the relocation. I didn't even know our destination.

Standing slightly apart from everyone, I noticed they were all geared up, gripping their duffle bags, dressed in combat-ready attire.

It struck me then—the kind of life I was getting deeper into. Despite the chaos, this unsettling shift was oddly comforting in its own twisted way. My apartment hadn't felt safe in ages.

My gaze drifted to a tall man with dark hair conversing with Zarek. His clean-shaven face revealed a noticeable scar on his jaw, adding a rugged aspect to his appearance. Nearby, Logan shared a joke, laughter echoing from him and another man who, although slightly shorter than Logan, still towered over most with a stature I guessed was over six feet. His skin was a rich brown, and he sported a neatly trimmed beard—perhaps he was Hispanic, or Indian?

God. But what a sight they made. All were ridiculously handsome, emanating deathly strength. They all had a hardened face, chiseled muscles, and biceps the size of my fucking waist.

"Don't let the looks fool you. They can kill with their bare hands," A woman appeared beside me, her voice pulling me out of my reverie. "Well, maybe not Kabir. He's a softie."

Standing a few inches taller than me, she had a presence that commanded attention. At five foot nine, I was hardly short, but next to her, I felt compelled to look up. Her dark-brown hair brushed just above her shoulders, and even in her tactical gear, it was clear she possessed a physique as capable and deadly as any member of the team.

I offered a hesitant smile, feeling slightly out of my element, "I'm not sure I know them enough to make any judgements."

She cocked her head, her gaze piercing as she studied me for a moment before extending her hand. "First, let me introduce myself. I'm Amelia Desmond. But they call me Amelia 'Falcon' Desmond. A call sign that stuck from my time in the FBI. I do surveillance and drone support for the squad."

Taking her hand, I felt the firmness of her grip, her strength subtly asserting itself. This woman wasn't just strong; she was formidable.

Or making a statement.

"Should you be telling me all this?" I asked.

She chuckled. "Well, I don't think you're going anywhere for a while. Boss won't let it happen."

"Would that be Zarek? The boss?"

She nodded, her gaze scrutinizing.

"In that case, maybe I should know a little about who I'll be spending my time with."

She smirked at my forwardness. Glancing towards Zarek and the imposing figure standing beside him, she continued. "That's Dylan 'Titan' Desmond. My brother and ex-CIA. Logan, Zarek, and Dylan were in the same special unit. They met there and never really separated, it seems."

Her nod shifted towards Logan and the other man, who I guessed was Kabir, sparking my curiosity about his call sign.

"And that softie, there, is Kabir 'Cipher' Gill. He worked with NASA's cybersecurity team and is our technology support. Hell of a hacker. But he goes in as a muscle every now and then."

"What are Zarek and Logan's call signs?" I asked,

intrigued.

"Oh, Zarek is 'Ghost'. Apparently he was very good at sneaking up on people on missions." Then she smirked at me, "Maybe not just on missions. And Logan is 'Gunner' because…well, he's good with guns. Knows everything about them."

She leaned in conspiratorially, "Don't tell him I said this, but the guy is a bit of a gun nerd. I'm sure he'd prefer a gun over a woman."

I stifled a laugh as I watched Logan enthusiastically showing his handgun to an unimpressed Kabir.

"FBI, CIA, and NASA." I mumbled. "What are you all doing in Canada? It seems like you're mostly American." I asked.

"We move around. We've only been here for three months. And we're not all American. Kabir is from India and Zarek's family is Canadian."

I nodded, following her as we approached the rest of the squad.

"Boys, ready to go?" Amelia called out.

A flurry of nods followed, and I watched as Amelia fell into step with Kabir, whispering something that made him shove her playfully. Moments later, I found myself in a Cadillac Escalade, tucked between an assortment of tactical gear.

Logan took the driver's seat, his eyes scanning the surroundings vigilantly as we waited for Zarek. I recalled our sparring session. He didn't seem so bad after a few punches. He even taught me how to block combinations and mix Krav Maga with kickboxing.

"I'm sorry we had to uproot your life like this." He mumbled suddenly.

I eyed him through the rearview mirror. "It's fine,

I guess. You didn't have to be rude, though."

He grimaced. "I was just taken aback. We don't bring civilians here. I'm sorry, for what it's worth."

"Logan, are you secretly the good cop?"

He chuckled. "Maybe. But I guess I can't mess with my boss's girl. He'd kick my ass."

I crossed my arms, a frown etching my features. "I'm not his anything."

Logan's smirk was visible in the mirror. "Aren't you?" His voice held a teasing lilt that I wasn't in the mood for.

I sighed, desperate to shift the conversation away from Zarek. "Can I call my friends and family? Let them know I'm okay?"

Logan's eyes met mine, his expression suddenly serious. "I think it's best to keep off the grid for now. We can pass along a message, but direct contact could put you—and them—at risk."

"Why?" My voice edged with frustration. "Why can't I just tell them I'm safe? I think they'd like to hear it from me."

"It's complicated," Logan started, his tone somber. "The squad is being watched. Any communication could lead them straight to you. Think of this as a sort of witness protection."

I scoffed, the reality of my situation sinking in. "You know I have a job, right? People expecting me back?"

His reply was curt, almost dismissive. "Do you?"

The implication of his words stung, the casual dismissal igniting a spark of anger. "What the hell is that supposed to mean?"

Logan's expression softened slightly. "Look, I know this is a lot to ask, but we need to play it safe for now. Trust me, it's for the best."

Before I could ask him to clarify what he meant, Zarek slid into the car and gave Logan a nod.

"You good?" he asked me.

You good? That's it? I'm literally in witness protection and he's asking me if I'm good.

"Peachy," I replied, the word dripping with sarcasm.

As we drove off, I tried to keep track of our route. But after almost forty minutes, my attention waned, and I surrendered to a nap.

The jarring sound of car doors opening yanked me back to consciousness.

"Hey Leo, wake up," Logan's voice called, a hint of amusement in his tone.

"Hey, are we there yet?" I mumbled, still half in the realm of sleep.

"Yes, we've reached. Get up and get inside now," Zarek cut in, his voice sharp and commanding.

His urgency allowed no time for a leisurely wake-up, and I found myself marching into what looked like a warehouse, my steps clumsy as I might have even stumbled.

"Can you be a bit gentle, asshole?" I heard Logan chastise Zarek, followed by a loud pat.

The building was a vast warehouse set in an isolated area, devoid of any other structures as far as the eye could see.

Inside, the main area was outfitted with gym equipment, a large table at the center, a modest kitchen to the left, and six doors that I presumed led to individual rooms.

Not long after, the second car rolled in, carrying Amelia, Dylan, and Kabir.

"Uh, I can shack up in the command center," Kabir suggested, already heading towards one of the rooms.

Zarek, silent until now, approached me from behind and took my hand, leading me toward two adjacent rooms. "This one is yours. I'm right next door if you need anything," he offered, his tone softening just slightly.

"If I need anything, I'll ask someone else," I retorted, my voice cold, as I forcefully opened the door to my room and hurried inside.

I threw my bag onto the bed and collapsed beside it, a move I instantly regretted. Pain shot through my ribs like a bolt of lightning, forcing a sharp yelp from my lips. Damn, my ribs weren't healed yet. I lay there for a few minutes, hoping the pain would ebb away, but it clung stubbornly.

Leaving my room, I knocked on a door I was certain wasn't Zarek's. Logan answered.

"Hey Leo!" He chirped.

"No one has ever called me Leo, Logan," I retorted with a roll of my eyes.

"Well, get used to it. What's up?"

"Do you have a painkiller?"

Before Logan could respond, Zarek's voice interrupted from behind me, "Why do you need a painkiller?"

"My ribs," I answered, directing my gaze solely at Logan, trying to avoid Zarek's probing eyes.

"Follow me," Zarek commanded, brushing past the awkwardness I was weaving around him. Logan gave a sympathetic shrug and closed his door.

✧ ✧ ✧

In Zarek's bedroom, he rifled through his shelf, returning with an ointment and a bottle of painkillers.

"You've been sparring while you were in pain?"

"Nope. Just landed on the bed wrong." I said, my response curt.

"You're upset with me." He concluded from the sharpness in my tone.

"No, I'm not."

"You can cuss me out, Leora. What I did—stalking you—was beyond wrong. I shouldn't have…fuck. I just knew that if something happened, it'd be my fault."

"I'm not upset about that. I understand why you did what you did." I blurted out.

He frowned in confusion. "So, you *are* upset about something."

"You want the truth, or the watered-down version of my anger?"

"Anger, huh? I want the truth. Always."

He gently lifted my shirt to apply the ointment on the bruising ribs that had turned a mottled blue-green. I tensed, not just from the cool ointment but from the contrasting heat of his touch.

"No one has seen my breasts in two years and three months. And then the one person who did was unaffected by them," I whispered, the words slipping out before I could catch them, my cheeks flushing with a mix of embarrassment and hurt. I closed my eyes, partly to hide my discomfort, partly because the cool touch of the ointment soothed the physical pain.

"Two years?" His tone was a mixture of curiosity and something else I couldn't quite place.

I bit my lip, opening my eyes to meet his. "Yes. It's been a long time."

"I wasn't... It's not that—"

"Please stop. You wanted the truth, I gave it." I cut him off, not ready to hear excuses or rationalizations.

He nodded and continued applying the ointment. His hand slightly slipped towards the edge of my breasts and I involuntarily gasped.

"I wasn't unaffected," he whispered, "I said I was trained to not get affected, but I failed miserably. I was more than just affected and I didn't want to be. You're a civilian, Leora. If anything happens, the squad will be dissolved."

"Why would anything happen if you're affected by my boobs? Make some sense." I scoffed weakly.

He shifted his position on the bed slightly and cupped my breasts, "If I'm affected, I'm compromised. If I'm compromised, I'm a liability. And a liability can get people killed."

"Then why were you stalking me?" I challenged him.

He blew out a harsh breath. "Because that was the closest I could get to you, without trapping you into this life."

"I'm here now. You couldn't stop that." I breathed out.

"I couldn't. But I'll get you back on track." He sounded defeated.

As his thumb brushed gently over my peaked nipple, a ripple of desire flickered across his expression–a yearning he was struggling to control.

"You're resisting this." I called him out.

"I am."

"Why?"

With his eyes shut, he answered. "None of us have significant others, Leora. And if…"

He remained silent.

"If what?"

He took a deep breath in and looked at me. "If you're it, which I think you might turn out to be, then I'm screwing over the squad, or worse, I'm dead."

His gaze softened and I whimpered when his hand squeezed my breast gently.

"Kiss me," I whispered.

His nostrils flared in anguish and he said the one word I dreaded, "No."

He slipped his hand out of my t-shirt, handed me the bottle of painkillers, and left the room. If embarrassed was how I felt the past few times Zarek rejected me, *this* felt like devastation. I had bluntly asked him, and he still left me yearning. A kiss wouldn't be enough to land him in the grave, would it?

Drop it, Leora. A few days, maybe weeks, and then you're out of his life.

I got up and left for my room.

ELEVEN

Zarek

I leaned against the kitchen counter, half-listening as Logan toyed with his food rather than eating it. Leora hadn't appeared all day, not for lunch, nor for dinner, and it was gnawing at my conscience. After giving her the painkillers, worry had started to eat at me—what if she had an allergic reaction?

"She should eat something," I muttered, more to myself, but Logan caught it.

He looked up, his eyebrow arching playfully. "What's up? Did you finally do something right or she's avoiding you out of shock?"

"Very funny," I retorted, not in the mood for his teasing. "I haven't done anything—well, not intentionally. I'm just concerned."

Logan's smirk widened as he pretended to examine his chicken wing closely. "Well, since you're playing stalker-nurse, you might want to know that Kabir found something interesting in her medical file. But maybe you don't need that stress."

"What?"

He shrugged and my patience snapped. "Logan, spit it out."

He sighed dramatically, putting down his food. "Okay, jeez. Two years ago, her ex-boyfriend stabbed her twice. She was in the hospital for three weeks."

The room seemed to tilt a little as his words sank in. Logan just nibbled at his chicken wing like he hadn't just obliterated my world.

I frowned. "Why are you only telling me this now?"

"Because you were too busy dying in guilt. Thought you might want to know why she's tougher than you think." Logan's tone softened.

I processed this, feeling a twinge of guilt.

"Thanks for the heads-up," I grumbled, not quite meeting his eyes.

"Don't thank me yet," Logan continued, "Thank her for not kicking your ass for being stupid. Go talk to her, Zarek. This is the woman you were stalking, man. That's gotta tell you something."

I found myself staring at Leora's closed door, piecing together the timeline. She hadn't been with anyone since that ex. That explained her stoicism, even when cleaning my wound that night—no flinch, no hesitation. A surge of guilt washed over me, constricting my chest painfully. Here she was, surviving, trying to change her world by becoming stronger, and what had I done? I had created an environment where she felt embarrassed and humiliated. A heavy sigh escaped me. My appetite vanished as I pushed my plate away, the food now tasteless.

✧ ✧ ✧

A sudden thud jolted me awake in the dead of night. Curious and a bit unsettled, I ventured out of my room only to spot a silhouette relentlessly pummeling a punching bag.

Leora.

I made my way over and quietly stationed myself behind the bag, holding it steady for her to prevent it from swinging wildly with each fierce punch.

"Go back to sleep," she grunted between strikes.

"This woke me up. I'm a light sleeper," I responded, my voice calm.

She paused, turning to face me with eyes full of fatigue and something darker, something wounded. "I heard what Logan told you. I knew your ultra-intelligent squad would eventually learn about it," her voice was thick with contempt.

I just keep screwing up with this woman.

"Leora, we just wanted to—"

"To what? Find out who I was? What I was hiding?" she interrupted, her voice rising slightly as she resumed her punching with renewed vigor.

"At least now I know and I can help in case—"

"Stop, Zarek. He's dead. And it's not a fucking weakness. I'm completely, absolutely, one hundred percent fine. I'm a psychologist, for fuck's sake. I just hate people knowing about it. *Hate it*. And you? You knowing, is more humiliating than you rejecting my kiss. What now? You want to kiss me now? Did it change your mind? Do you pity me now?" Her sequence of strikes—straight, uppercut, hook—was relentless.

I straightened my spine, holding the punching bag

firmly, meeting her fury with a steady gaze. "When I kiss you, not if, *when* I fucking take that mouth of yours, Leora Mateez, it will have nothing to do with anything but me claiming you. You understand?"

The intensity of my words seemed to freeze both of us in place. I hadn't expected to say that. Why the fuck was I giving her hope?

I saw the shock, the conflict, the defiance all flicker in her eyes. She tore away her wraps, and without another word, turned on her heel and retreated to her room.

TWELVE

Leora

"Teach me how to shoot a gun," I declared to Logan the next morning. I didn't want to be a sitting duck. I needed to do something. Help the squad and not be a liability to them.

"Ex-CIAs, ex-FBI, ex-NASA cybersecurity, hell, I even guarded the Pope once. We don't need your help, Leo," Logan retorted with a dismissive wave.

"Teach. Me. I've been to a shooting range before. I'll be a good student."

"Why?"

"I need to be able to protect myself? Is that reason good enough?"

"Fine!" Logan exhaled, his annoyance giving way to a reluctant smile.

We made our way to the back of the warehouse where Logan set up a makeshift range with empty beer bottles as targets. He handed me a Luger Kel-Tec, its compact form fitting snugly in my hand. "It's a pocket gun, with minimal recoil. But still, be careful," he instructed, pointing out the features. "It's double action, no manual safety. Just point and shoot."

"Point and shoot," I repeated under my breath, adopting a stance I'd seen countless times in films. I noticed Logan's smirk out of the corner of my eye and shook my head, determined to focus.

I aimed at the left-most beer bottle and fired. The bottle shattered spectacularly into pieces. Rather than celebrate, I steeled myself and quickly took down the next target, and the next, until all five were demolished.

"I guess you don't need me to teach you how to aim," Logan chuckled, impressed.

"Was it a fluke?" I asked, hoping it wasn't.

"Well, let's see," he said, picking up another bottle and placing it on his head as he stood back at the target area, a mischievous grin playing on his lips.

What the fuck?

I shook my head swiftly, but he just smiled wider.

Well, fuck it.

"Your funeral," I shouted, half-joking, half-serious, and took aim at the bottle perched precariously on his head.

The shot rang out, and the bottle exploded, leaving Logan unscathed. I exhaled a shaky breath of relief, quickly walked up to him, and punched him in the gut.

"You're fucking crazy! What if I had actually shot you?"

"It wasn't a fluke when you shot five bottles in a row, Leo." He laughed, dodging the additional punches I threw in mock anger.

Deep down, I felt liberated. It was as though the

fragmented pieces of my life were snapping into place, forming a coherent picture after years of chaos. This rush, this pulse of life—it was something I hadn't truly felt in far too long.

"Get back inside, you morons. We have incoming, code yellow," Amelia yelled from the corner of the warehouse.

"Aah fuck me!" Logan sighed and slowly started walking back to the warehouse.

"Shouldn't you hurry?"

"Code yellow, the threat is more than twelve hours away. Code red, the threat is here breathing down our necks. Capiche?"

"Got it," I smiled as I followed him back into the warehouse.

✧ ✧ ✧

"Squad Two was hit, we've lost three of the members. Brewer is alive, barely," Kabir announced as Logan and I walked back in. His voice carried a trace of his Indian accent, though it was gradually melding into an American one. He sat at the table, his laptop open before him. Amelia hovered behind, her eyes scanning the screen over his shoulder.

"Who did we lose?" Zarek asked, his voice steady as he methodically loaded his magazines and strapped on his vest.

"Kaylan, Kyle, and..." Kabir's voice trailed off. He glanced up at Dylan, his expression crumbling, "Fuck."

"Kabir?" Zarek pressed, urgency lacing his tone.

"It was Riley," Amelia interjected softly, her voice barely a whisper. She abruptly stood, walked over to the punching bag, and unleashed a ferocious punch against it.

Dylan's breathing hitched, his frame rigid as tears glossed over his eyes. Logan moved to his side, placing a supportive hand on his shoulder.

"What am I missing?" I whispered to Zarek, feeling suddenly outside the circle of grief.

"Riley was Dylan's..." Zarek paused, his eyes shutting as if to block out the pain, "She was Dylan's."

Watching Dylan, a mountain of a man, his emotions warping his features into a visage of agony, stirred something deep within me. He stormed off to his room, the door slamming with a force.

And in that moment, a selfish part of me was relieved—relieved that Zarek wasn't mine to lose in such a way.

"Squad Six, officially report for interception sequence," Zarek's command broke through the heavy air.

"Fuck. Carlton 35543 reporting active, show me go," Logan responded, his voice firm.

"Rivera 32577 reporting active, show me go," Zarek added.

"Desmond 39901 reporting active, show me go," Amelia's voice was thick but determined.

"Gill 34249 reporting active, show me go," Kabir followed.

Dylan reemerged, his demeanor hardened, a stark transformation from moments before. "Desmond 39900 reporting active, show me go."

"Dyl, sit this one out, man. It's fine," Logan tried to dissuade him.

"Show. Me. Go." Dylan's glare was resolute, directed at both Zarek and Logan. I was slowly coming to realize that the squad members had a troubling habit of masking their fears and grief.

Zarek then turned to me, his expression grave. "Stay here, stay hidden. Do not go outside unless the safehouse is compromised. The alarm system will be engaged, and if there's a breach, we will be informed."

"I'm leaving my Luggie with her," Logan handed over his gun to me, his nod conveying trust. "She can aim."

As he began to gear up, Zarek took my hand and led me to his room, closing the door behind us. He pulled out a bulletproof vest from under the bed, tossed it over my head, and began fastening the straps.

"Be very, *very* careful. You'll be by yourself."

"I can take care of myself," I asserted, trying to match his intensity.

He cupped my cheeks gently, his touch a stark contrast to our usual interactions. We seemed to have put our animosity on hold for now. Kissing my brows, he pressed his forehead against mine.

"Everything will be fine," he murmured, his breath warm against my lips.

"Are you saying that for me, or for yourself?" I asked.

"Probably myself."

A small smile took over my face. "Everything will be fine, Zarek." I finally echoed.

After one last reassuring gaze, he steered us back to the hall to join the others.

THIRTEEN

Zarek

"We all know our assignments and positions. It's basic interception and retrieval of goods. Shoot to maim only. Let's go!" My voice echoed commandingly through the warehouse.

"Yes, boss!" Logan responded with a playful salute.

As we all moved toward the main exit, fully geared in our vests and masks, I couldn't help but steal a glance back at Leora. There she stood, somehow radiant even in the starkness of a tank top, vest, and shorts. The thought of leaving her alone left a familiar ache in my chest.

Our eyes met, and a jolt of electricity seemed to surge through the space between us.

"Fuck it." The word slipped from my lips before I even realized I'd spoken. I paced back towards her, yanking down my mask as I closed the distance. Once she was within reach, I grabbed her by the waist, pulling her forcefully toward me, and captured her mouth with mine.

It felt like I finally had the answer to all my questions. Why had I stalked her? Why was I obsessed with her?

This. This is why.

I was melting into her when her lips parted, welcoming me in. Diving into the kiss, my tongue explored hers in an enchanting dance. It was a punishing, consuming kiss that left us both gasping for air, her hands traveled to my neck, pulling me closer. She moaned into the kiss, a sound so profoundly beautiful it shattered all my defenses. At that moment, I was utterly lost, and *hell*, I didn't want to be found.

Too soon, the necessity of the moment forced us to part.

I kissed her once more, gently this time, a stark contrast to the fierce urgency of our first. Reluctantly turning away, I rejoined my squad by the door. Logan smirked and tossed the car keys to me, his wink at Leora both teasing and knowing.

I shot him a glare. Opening the door, I stepped out, haunted by the thought that this fervent, stolen kiss might be the first and last with Leora for many reasons.

✧ ✧ ✧

"No one's here." Logan's voice came through the earpiece.

Amelia and I were stationed in a three-bedroom detached house, strategically positioned half a block from Crazon's drop-off location. Meanwhile, Kabir, Dylan, and Logan were on point for the interception, with us ready as backup.

"I have eyes on an armored truck at the south entrance of the target house." Amelia reported, her eyes glued to the drone feed on her laptop.

"They're here. I repeat, shoot to maim, gather the goods, and get the hell out. The goods are what we're here for," I directed my next statement to the one person I thought could be reckless, "Titan, you hear me? We don't need hostages to question."

There was silence for a good five seconds before Dylan's rough voice came through, "Copy."

"I see two heat signatures, Gunner. One on the porch, one inside, six meters from the door," she relayed.

"Copy," Logan uttered.

I saw a scuffle happen between two dots in her laptop.

"Front porch clear. Cipher and Gunner are a go," *Logan*.

"Titan providing cover," *Dylan*.

A few minutes passed by, and after a few gunshots, I heard a long silence.

"Gunner, clear, unhit, on extraction." *Logan*.

"Cipher, clear, unhit, on extraction." *Kabir*.

The silence that followed was thicker, tenser. Then it was shattered by a strained report, "Titan, unclear, incapacitated, near north entrance."

As soon as Dylan's pained voice cut through the earpiece, a curse slipped from my lips. Amelia's face drained of color, her eyes widened in shock, and her lips trembled.

I let out a heavy, erratic sigh and took command, "Ghost, engaging, rescuing Titan."

"Got your six, Ghost," Logan said.

"Falcon, get on extraction and support Cipher," I said.

When she didn't move, I grabbed her by her shoulders and gave her an affirming nod, "Your brother's fine, Amelia. He's alive. I'll bring him back."

She nodded, her eyes quickly blinking away the fear as she unholstered her gun and rushed out through the back exit.

Giving myself a moment to collect my thoughts, I sprinted towards the target house, an old, mansion-sized Victorian. An unconscious guard lay on the porch as I entered.

Inside, I searched for Dylan. A man lay sprawled near the entryway, clearly injured but still a threat as his eyes met mine and he fired. I dodged, taking cover behind a couch, then moved quietly towards him.

Shots whizzed by. Another shot. And another.

I rose and returned fire.

Logan burst in from the back, diving and sliding towards the assailant. He grabbed the man by the neck, cutting off his blood supply with a precise chokehold.

"Thanks, Gunner," I acknowledged with a nod as Logan smiled back.

"Fucking nineteen!" He boasted, referring to the countless times he'd been my savior since the CIA.

I waved him off.

As soon as I saw movement near the kitchen, I strode towards it stealthily. A man with dark hair lay on the floor in a pool of blood.

Dylan. Fuck.

Adrenaline surged as I ran to him, lifting the formidable bulk of his body onto my shoulder, and made a dash for the exit.

"Just like old times, Ghost," he whispered.

"Don't speak."

Once I reached the surveillance house half a block away, adrenaline still pumping, I hoisted Dylan onto the dining table, an impromptu operating surface. Ripping open a box of first aid supplies, I frantically scattered gauze, skin glue, and medical tape across the surface. "I got you, Dyl," I murmured, part reassurance, part promise.

Quickly, I stripped him of his vest and located the wound just below his collarbone. A guttural scream tore from Dylan's throat as I peeled back his shirt, revealing the damage.

"Through and through, Titan. You're good," I assessed aloud, trying to inject a bit of confidence into the grim situation as I began the patch-up job.

"Report status, Gunner," I called through the earpiece, my hands steady as I worked.

"Six of their men hit, five unconscious, one dead. House is clear. Shipment secure in our Escalade. How's Dyl?" Logan's voice crackled through, business as usual.

"He's fine, lost a bunch of blood. Falcon, get back here for assist," I said.

I didn't really need help. But I knew Amelia wanted to see her brother alive and breathing. A few minutes later she ran back in, cupped his cheeks and smiled.

"There's no 901 without 900, brother," she whispered in his ear.

"There's no," Dylan let out a heavy breath, "900 without 901, sister."

"Glad you're not dead." She turned to me then. "What do you need?"

"All set," I patched him with skin glue, put a gauze on him and taped him up. "There. Done!"

Amelia shook her head, a small smile playing on her lips as she looked at Dylan, a silent exchange of sibling love passing between them.

"Let's go back, squad," I stated.

"Back to the lovely Leora, I see?" Logan's voice teased through the earpiece, a chuckle softening the edges of a tense day.

"Read the room, Gunner," I muttered, rolling my eyes even though he couldn't see.

FOURTEEN

Leora

The wait was intolerable. Every minute stretched endlessly, each tick of the clock amplifying my fears. What if they were injured? What if they never returned?

I desperately needed a way to communicate with them.

As I paced the confines of my room, thoughts of Zarek haunted me. The prospect of never seeing him again, of never feeling his kiss, was crushing. Each shared look, every moment together had deepened my affection for him, drawing me deeper into an emotional whirlpool.

Before joining this life, I had drifted aimlessly, merely distracting myself enough to live 'normally'.

Yet, this new life, this new purpose with Zarek and the squad, brought clarity. It resonated with a part of me that I hadn't known was seeking direction.

I was not meant to be a passive observer in my own life. I needed to be involved, to be part of the narrative that was unfolding. My previous life, especially these past two years, felt like being forced to swim with bound hands—I refused to experience that helplessness again.

With a deep, steadying breath, I made a decision. It was time to take action. The thought of contributing actively, of fighting alongside Zarek and the others, ignited something within me. Although I was not fully privy to their mission's specifics, I figured that I would be soon.

The sound of an engine slicing through the quiet triggered an immediate reaction in me. I darted toward the door, my heart hammering with the desperate hope that Zarek and the squad were returning unscathed.

Kabir entered first, and my gaze quickly swept over him, scanning for injuries. Aside from a few cuts on his face, he seemed intact. Relief washed over me briefly until my eyes caught the sight of Logan and Zarek supporting Dylan between them. Dylan's t-shirt was pulled up over his shoulder, revealing a large patch of gauze just below his collarbone.

"Is he okay?" I asked, my voice tight with concern as I looked from Zarek to Dylan. "Are you okay, Dylan?"

"Fantastic. Getting shot for the fifteenth time now," Dylan quipped with a weary smile that didn't quite reach his eyes.

"Oh God!" The words escaped me as a whisper.

I helped them escort Dylan to his room. Once done, I shifted towards Zarek and leaned slightly.

"Can we talk?" I asked.

He nodded.

"I need him resting," he commanded as we moved to his room. As he shut the door behind us, he began to shed his vest, his movements heavy with fatigue.

"I can't be the helpless woman waiting at home for her military man," I blurted out, the words tumbling out in a rush.

He stiffened, pausing mid-motion. I felt as though something had irreversibly changed within him, between the kiss this morning and now. Without meeting my gaze, he murmured, "I see. What do you want, then?"

"You need to train me. I need to learn to be part of the squad," I declared, my voice firm.

Disbelief flickered across his face. "You're not—it doesn't work like that."

"Tell me how and I'll do it," I insisted, meeting his hesitant gaze.

"Where is this even coming from?"

I took a step towards him. "I have felt this way since the night in the alley."

"Felt what?" He asked.

"Just… me needing to be a part of something more. My life felt robotic before. And I want to feel useful here."

He looked at me, puzzled. "You want to be a part of this squad?" His words came out slow, as if needing his own confirmation.

"Yes."

He looked away, his shoulders slumping. "I'll have to talk to higher ups about recruiting you. There's a written test. You need to train to pass a mock mission and get your physical and mental exams done." He graced me with a pained look. "It's not easy."

"Okay. I can try at least. I will lose my job at the Detention Centre for being absent without cause. I have nothing to do until this case closes."

"Leora, this isn't a life you want. It's dangerous. You saw what happened to Squad Two. Dylan barely made it out today. And the mock mission isn't really mock. People die in those."

"I know what I want. And I've worked with criminals before. I want to help and not be helpless when I'm being targeted," I countered, my resolve steeling.

He looked at me, his gaze burning. "No. You're not doing this. Once this case is closed and we've got the tail off your back, you're going back to your life. This isn't what you should want. I didn't save you, only to get you killed on a fucking *mission*."

"Did you not hear me? I can't be that helpless woman—"

"*'Waiting for your military man.'* I got it," he interrupted, his voice suddenly distant. "You don't have to, you know?"

"What?" My voice cracked, a sharp stab of pain threading through it as I anticipated where this was leading.

"You don't have to wait for me. I might not even come back one day."

"Are you serious? Wasn't it just this morning when you quote unquote *claimed* me?" My breathing became erratic.

"That may have been an oversight on my part."

"Oversight," I laughed without humor.

"Leora, you can't want this. You have a life, you have friends and family. You're not thinking straight."

"Oh," I nodded, a bitter edge to my voice. "Send

me back then." I challenged.

"As I said," he shook his head, "you're not thinking straight."

"So, let me get this straight. You won't train me. You refuse to kiss me. I'm off-limits to you. And now I can't even pull my weight with the squad?" My voice rose with every accusation. "Right? That's what you're saying? That I stay fucking helpless?"

"That's not—"

"Right?" My voice grew louder.

Zarek closed his eyes, his features tightening as if my words physically pained him. "Yes. I don't want you to be a part of this squad."

"Take. Me. Back." The words came out sharp, my teeth clenched in frustration.

He rose swiftly, his movements brimming with a tense, intimidating energy as he closed the distance between us. "And then what?" he gritted through his teeth, "You get kidnapped? *Again?* They use you to get to us? *Again?* You want to risk my squad's lives for meaningless rescue ops?"

His glare was unyielding, and it dawned on me then. Hell, I was *meaningless* to him. A liability. I sucked in a ragged breath and turned away.

"Fuck, I didn't mean—" he began, his tone shifting, but I didn't stay to hear the rest. I stormed out of his room, the door slamming behind me.

FIFTEEN

Zarek

Fuck. Fucking fuck!

I had screwed up. The hurt I saw flicker in her eyes—the hurt I caused—it was not something I could shake off.

I called her rescue mission from when she was kidnapped, *meaningless*, when it had meant *everything* to me.

Just as the echo of the door slam faded, Logan burst into my room. His entrance was less a question, more an accusation. "What the fuck did you do now?" He demanded.

"Stay out of this, Log—"

"She wants me to drive her back to Toronto," he cut in, his tone a mix of disbelief and irritation. "Says if I don't, she'll sneak out herself. Obviously, she won't manage, but what the hell, man?"

"Fuck!" My hands went to my hair, pulling at the roots as if I could somehow yank the frustration right out of my skull. I recounted the disastrous conversation to Logan, who listened in silence, his expression unreadable.

After a heavy pause, he finally spoke. "Listen, Zar. If she wants to train, let her. If she thinks she can handle a mission, start her on surveillance with Amelia. Maybe even talk to Callahan about getting her into the training program."

"She's a civilian!" I exploded, the word 'civilian' sounding more like an accusation than a fact.

"So were we, once," Logan countered calmly, leaning against the door frame. "I don't think anything about her decision has to do with you. It's probably about that ex of hers, Adriano."

The mention of that bastard Adriano's name ignited a familiar rage within me. "Adriano McLeen, that motherf—"

"Can't kill a dead man, Zarek," Logan interjected, his voice flat.

I sighed, the fight draining out of me as reality set in. "Fine, train her. But I'm not talking to Alpha One about this," I said. "And make sure it's just self-defense. She is *not* part of the squad," I added, fixing him with a hard glare.

"Fine," Logan agreed, a bit too quickly.

"Fine," I spat.

"Fine," he threw his hands up in exasperation. "Jeez, chill!" He shook his head as he left the room, leaving me to stew in regret.

✧ ✧ ✧

I glanced over as Logan toyed with one of the Crazons we'd snagged yesterday. Morning light poured into the warehouse, casting long shadows. "Looks like a disc of soap, doesn't it?" he chuckled, tossing it lightly between his hands.

"Hey, careful with that," Kabir warned, his eyes narrowing. "I've shut off any external tracking they might've placed on it, but who knows if it's got some sort of beacon we haven't found yet."

Logan examined the Crazon, his finger hovering over the discreet power button etched into the back. "Not planning to start a fireworks show, are you, Gunner?" I chimed in, half-joking.

He rolled his eyes at us, setting the Crazon back on the metal table with a soft clank. Stretching his arms above his head, he announced, "Alright, training calls." He waved nonchalantly and sauntered out, the door clanging shut behind him.

Kabir shot me a look as the echo faded. "Are we really bringing in a trainee now?"

Amelia, leaning against a nearby stack of crates, grinned. "I wouldn't mind some female energy around here."

I sighed, rubbing the bridge of my nose. "It's just for self-defense, not full squad training," I clarified, "And just for the record, it wasn't my idea."

"Of course not. The mighty old Zarek would never endanger a woman by training her. Lest she learn how to take care of herself. No, no! Mighty Zarek needs to be the protector," Amelia drawled animatedly.

"What did I ever do to you?" I grumbled.

"Zarek, please. On my first day, you put me on surveillance, and I am still on it. I'm more of a combat operative than Kabir, yet here I am. Sur-*fucking*-veillance."

"Hey!" Kabir slapped her arm lightly as she eyed him with a *tell me I'm wrong, I dare you* look.

"Did you just imply I'm sexist?" I rolled my eyes, "You're a trained surveillance and drone expert. Yes, you've fought *two* combat missions. But, I put you where your expertise lies."

"Fine, I won't argue with that. I'm an expert after all." She smiled.

My lips twitched, not enough to call it a smile, but Amelia's smile widened.

"Did you talk to her after your fight?" She asked. Kabir pretended not to listen and continued to work on his laptop.

"We didn't fight."

"The walls are pretty thin, Boss," Kabir muttered.

"Great, so you all heard."

"Just the bits that were loud enough," Amelia grinned.

I remained quiet, my face blank. I didn't need my squad thinking I was distracted.

"What's the estimate on testing? I want to know what this soap thing is," I asked Kabir.

"0 minutes and 45 seconds," he squinted at his screen mockingly.

"Amelia, get started when he's ready."

I left the team to start their testing and went to check on Dylan who was still resting on heavy painkillers. I saw him sound asleep as I opened his door slightly, and then quickly shut it to avoid disturbing him.

Leaving Dylan to rest, I made my way back to my room. I didn't want to start working out and relieving this tension right in front of my squad. Dropping down, I started doing a few pushups. My mind was reeling, replaying the conversation with Leora. It churned in my mind, her determination clashing with my concerns. She could be killed, dammit.

Late into the night, the familiar thud of fists against the punching bag drew me from my room. With a reluctant pause, I made my way to the makeshift gym where Leora was taking out her frustrations on the bag.

"Use your shoulder blades more," I advised quietly, immediately regretting it as her glare pinned me like a sharp dagger.

"Use my shoulder blades." She scoffed, a harsh laugh breaking through her controlled exterior. "And when will you stop controlling my life?"

"Leora—"

"No!" The word sliced through the air. "When will you stop dictating what I should or shouldn't do?"

Her reaction cut deep, laying bare the core of her frustration. She stepped away from the punching bag, her movements bristling with anger, and strode towards the long table at the center of the warehouse. With a sharp gesture, she ripped off her gloves and slammed them down.

I followed her, my own frustration mounting but my voice remained steady, "Why, Leora? Why is joining the squad so important to you?"

"Why?" she echoed, her tone laced with exasperation. "Because I want to know what it's like to be needed, to do something that makes others feel safe."

"I get it—"

"No, Zarek, you *don't*." Her interruption was sharp, and she looked up, her eyes softening despite her anger. "I've been dealt shitty hands over and over. *I've* never felt safe. I need this. I need to feel capable, Zarek. I can't sit around and let people dictate my life. I have had that life before. With Adriano. You know all about him, don't you?"

I closed my eyes in frustration. "I don't know everything."

"There's not much to tell. Just a series of bad decisions because I was too naive to see that when others impose their will, dictate your life, it leads to nothing but trouble. When they assume they know better, they're not protecting you—they're fucking sentencing you."

Her words hit hard, and an uncomfortable silence fell between us. I struggled to keep my composure, my fury raging. "Are you saying I'm like *him*?"

Her eyes met mine, fierce yet filled with a pleading for understanding. "Zarek, every time you try to decide what's best for me without listening, it feels the same."

The torrent of emotions swirling within me was almost unbearable. Leora's comparison of me to that vile ex of hers triggered a volcanic anger inside me, and I couldn't see past the haze of red clouding my vision. I stalked toward her, my strides deliberate and menacing, trapping her against the edge of the table with a ferocity that mirrored my inner turmoil. My voice was a low growl. "You want me? You want this squad? Have at it, woman!"

Her eyes met mine, a fiery determination burning within them. "Yes, I want it," she whispered, her voice steady despite the storm around us.

In an instant, my lips crashed against hers, our mutual fury transforming into a desperate, searing kiss. I lifted her effortlessly, setting her on the table without breaking the kiss, her fingers weaving through my hair while her other hand explored the contours of my bare chest.

When we finally broke for air, her hands fumbled with the drawstrings of my sweatpants. My response was immediate and primal; I yanked at the fabric of her leggings, ripping them apart at the seams, thankful in that reckless moment that she wore nothing underneath.

She deftly pulled my sweatpants down, her gaze locked on my hard length with an intensity that matched her earlier fervor. She aligned me with her, and with one forceful thrust, I was enveloped in her warmth. "Fuck, baby," I rasped, my forehead resting against hers, overwhelmed by how she was squeezing me, "you're so fucking tight. Two years, huh?"

"Two fucking years, Zarek. Now *move*!"

I smirked against her lips, starting with slow, deliberate strokes that soon quickened into a relentless pace. As I lavished her neck with kisses, her moans filled the air, vibrating against my lips. My hand found her clit, teasing and pinching, driving her towards a climax.

The world seemed to shrink to the raw, visceral connection between us. Her climax was fierce, pulling me deeper into her as her body clamped around mine.

I lost myself in her warmth, watching as a vivid blush spread from her cheeks down her neck, tinting the skin visible above her camisole. She was breathtaking, completely undone and beautifully spent.

Driven by her response, I chased my own release, which overtook me with shattering intensity.

Blinking through my dazed haze, I kissed her,

hard. As we both came down from the high, reality began to seep back in. "Fuck, I didn't use—"

"I'm clean," she interrupted, her smile wistful. "And I had a shot recently."

I exhaled in relief. "I'm clean too. Not much action on that front with all the missions," I said.

"What, no other women you stalked?" She asked, her eyes gleaming with playfulness.

But then the gravity of what just happened hit me. I knew I couldn't have this.

Why the hell did we do this?

This was a mistake. Despite the intensity of what we shared, I knew it was wrong. She was a civilian; I couldn't let her be dragged deeper into my world. She had to remain safe. She could still go back to her old life.

Keeping my eyes shut, perhaps too cowardly to face her reaction, I finally spoke the words I knew would make her loathe me. "This shouldn't have happened, Leora."

"What?" Her soft whimper started poking through my defenses.

Keep it together, Zar.

She pushed me back gently, and I moved away several steps, adjusting my sweatpants. "We shouldn't have done this. It doesn't mean what you think it means." *I shouldn't have let it get this far.*

Her silence was heavy, filled with confusion and hurt—a stark contrast to the passion just moments before. As I looked into her eyes, filled with emerging tears, I knew I had not only crossed a line but also hurt someone who had begun to mean more to me than I dared admit.

"You coward!" Leora hissed through her tears and

walked away. I stood there, frozen. The only sound surrounding me was my shattered breath, broken just like me.

SIXTEEN

Zarek

It really wasn't a good look on me—this mix of misery, anger, and impatience was unbecoming of a squad leader. Yet, that's what painted my days lately. I snapped at Logan over his harmless jokes and dismissed Amelia's pointed observations with barely a second thought. The team sensed the shift; they could feel the icy divide and, without much fuss, they lined up behind Leora, silently taking her side against mine.

Why couldn't they see? Why were they so eager to drag someone else into this maelstrom of danger and uncertainty? I knew too well what happened when people got tangled up in the affairs meant for those in the Alpha program. We were hardened by training, both mentally and physically, prepared for anything—or so we told ourselves. Our only family was the squad; we had long given up on the illusion of a normal life. What was so noble about pulling someone else into this life?

It wasn't just about keeping her safe anymore; it was about the raw fear that gripped me whenever I thought of her facing the dangers we lived with daily.

I couldn't understand her point of view. And I couldn't make her understand mine. Until it all came rushing back and I could no longer keep my fears from her.

✧ ✧ ✧

"Zar!" Zavier's familiar voice chirped from the backyard. "Check this out!"

I was visiting home after my second tour as the Alpha Squad Six member. My brother had barely seen me in the past few years.

I was in one of my rather solemn moods. We had lost a member of our Squad, Maxton. We couldn't even get his body transferred back to his family. I was beyond exhausted with my appeals to Bridgewood.

Dragging myself from the sofa, I found my way to where Zavier was lounging on the patio bench, his enthusiasm a stark contrast to my gloom.

"Look at this." He waved his phone at me, his face lit up like a kid with a new toy. He shoved the screen in my face, an email blinking back that spoke of recruitment opportunities with the CIA right at his precinct. "It's a covert hire, man. Can you believe it?"

"That's incredible, Z." I managed, shoving aside my own dark cloud for a moment to bask in his excitement. "You thinking about talking to the Chief?"

"Yeah, I mean, I've had enough of playing shepherd to lost elderly folk from the retirement homes around the precinct," he groaned, rolling his eyes dramatically. "Every day it's another wild goose chase for someone who's wandered off. I can't do it

anymore, Zar."

I couldn't help but chuckle; his frustrations might have seemed trivial to me once, but they were his daily battles. "You want out to chase bigger things, huh?"

"Exactly! I mean, you're out there, doing important stuff with the CIA. Maybe one day we'll even team up on a mission or something, right?" His grin was all the sunshine I needed, and I didn't have the heart to tell him that I was no longer CIA.

"I hear you, Z. But remember, it's not all action and glory. It's a lot of missed family dinners, and yeah, they might not even keep you stateside."

He nodded, the weight of my words sinking in, but the sparkle didn't quite leave his eyes. He was ready, maybe for the adventure, maybe to step out of his big brother's shadow.

Just then, our dad's voice boomed, "Zavier!" signaling his return from wherever he'd been pottering about.

I nudged Zavier with my elbow. "Come on, let's go surprise him, he doesn't know I'm home."

And just like that, we headed toward Dad, who was utterly unaware of our approach. The sight of me made his hands falter, and the bag he was holding tumbled to the ground, its contents spilling out unceremoniously.

"Zarek, my boy!" His voice boomed as he rushed over, his arms enveloping me in one of those robust, back-thumping hugs that I'd almost forgotten in my time away. "Hey, Dad!" I managed, the familiarity of home wrapping around me like a warm blanket.

"What are you doing here?" He pulled back, his eyes wide with surprise. "I thought Nuria had you this time of year."

The mention of my mother's name sliced through the moment like a cold breeze. The divorce hadn't been kind, leaving scars too deep and too raw; Dad had moved us from Canada to the USA when I was twelve, creating a chasm between us and Mom that never really healed.

I hadn't seen her much over the years, a silent accord sealed by the choices made back then—that we were unequivocally Dad's kids, not Nuria's. She was a woman who had loved deeply, fiercely even, sometimes standing between us and Dad when things got too intense. But Zavier had chosen Dad, and as the older brother, I'd felt it my duty to uphold his decision, to protect him, even if it meant leaving behind a part of ourselves.

The weekend unfolded with a sense of normalcy I hadn't felt in years, spending time with Zavier and Dad, just like old times. There was a comforting thought that soon, Zavier might join me in my line of work, bringing us even closer. The idea of sharing more of my life with him, perhaps easing the isolation my job often imposed, seemed almost soothing.

What I didn't anticipate was that only six months later, I would be standing at the edge of a grave, shoveling dirt onto a casket. That I'd be carrying the weight of pushing my brother into my world only to lose him in his first real assignment. That I'd never forgive myself for letting my brother join the CIA.

✧ ✧ ✧

"Who is this?"

Leora's voice broke through the haze of my grief, her presence a sudden clarity in my bedroom as I clutched the picture of Zavier—a token I kept hidden behind my decoy badge holder. My hands shook, the image wavering as if threatened by the very air around us.

"Zavier," my voice cracked, a name that seemed to ache with everything I had lost. "My brother."

"You have a brother?" Her voice was gentle, a tentative step into my guarded world.

I could only nod, the truth twisting in me. "Had," I corrected, the word falling like a stone in the stillness of the room. "Not anymore."

Her expression shifted from curiosity to something deeper, more poignant. "Oh, Zarek…"

"It's fine," I lied, sliding the photo back into its hiding place behind my badge. "Just…don't want to add another picture to the collection."

Leora exhaled slowly, her gaze never wavering from mine, reading me as if I were pages in a book she could somehow understand. "I can't erase your fears, Zarek. Just like you can't erase mine."

I nodded, the gesture heavy, burdened. "He was a good cop, you know? Wanted to be more like me." The words tasted bitter, filled with irony and regret.

Her attention was unwavering as I continued, the dam inside me breaking. "He joined the CIA, thought it was his calling. Was good at it, too—trained hard, got deployed fast." My voice broke with the weight of what came next. "First mission out, they walked right into an ambush. A mole in their unit led them straight to a group named, Deathmark." My throat tightened around the words. "They didn't stand a chance."

"I'm sorry, Zarek," she whispered.

I shook my head, dismissing her sympathy with a bitter smile. After Z's death, my relationship with both my parents soured. He was the golden child. And suddenly, I wasn't enough. They couldn't look at me the same. I was the one who encouraged him, after all.

"So, now you know why I can't let you do this." I whispered.

She watched me, her eyes filled with a quiet strength. "I'm not him, Zarek," she said, her voice firm. "Your fears are real, yes. But they're yours, Zarek. Don't make them mine."

Her words struck deep, a reminder of the burdens I carried—not just for myself, but for those I tried to protect, perhaps too fiercely. In her eyes, I saw not just understanding, but a plea for freedom—the freedom to face her own battles. The silence was deafening. But neither of us broke it.

After a few silent beats, she got up and left.

SEVENTEEN

Zarek

The next day I made my way out to the back of the warehouse that Logan had converted into a mini-bootcamp. Targets lay across the field and when I squinted hard enough, I saw that the target paper had a face that was quite familiar.

Logan grinned as Leora shot through my nose, or rather a print of my face.

"Funny," I said dryly. "Burn them when you're done, jackass!"

Leora was moving across the field executing a multi-position shooting drill. She didn't hit the target every time, but I had to admit, she was damn good for a rookie. After two sprints, she switched magazines effortlessly and continued. I watched her, completely mesmerized by her grace and skill. After two more five-shot sprints she paused and looked up at Logan who was clapping.

"Good job, Leo. That's a score of 12 out of 20. I'm impressed," he said. She smiled widely and looked back to see me staring at her.

Her smile faltered, and in a move that caught me completely off guard, she swiftly switched out the magazine, cocked the gun, and aimed it straight at me. My eyebrows knitted together in confusion, yet I remained motionless.

I'd stared down the barrel of a gun more times than I could count, but nothing had prepared me for this—Leora, with a blend of fury and pain etching her features, pointing a gun at me.

Fuck, I'd even let her shoot me. I stepped closer, the gun's cold muzzle pressing against my chest.

"I'm sorry. In case it's the last thing I say," I murmured softly.

After a tense moment, her arm fell to her side. She turned towards Logan, shielding her eyes from the harsh sunlight, and declared flatly, "I'm hungry."

Logan's chuckle echoed faintly, but my focus remained fixed on Leora as she walked away. The sound of her steps crunching the grass beneath her feet slowly faded into silence. Rooted to the spot, I felt as if my legs were made of concrete. I didn't have the strength to follow her, to move, to do anything. My apology had left me with nothing but the cold shoulder of her searing ignorance. A heavy sigh escaped my lips as I turned away.

By the time I looked back, Logan and Leora had already disappeared inside. That's when the distant sound of a car door snapping shut cut through the quiet, pulling a frown across my face. We were miles from any semblance of civilization; whoever was here was definitely out of place. A prickling sensation crawled up the back of my neck, and then it happened—the unmistakable crack of a shot and a searing pain ripped through my right arm as a bullet grazed me.

"Fuck."

Instinctively, I dove for cover behind one of Logan's makeshift barriers, pulling out my SIG as I did. My phone vibrated against my thigh. I took it out hastily and Logan's name flashed on the screen.

"Unidentified sniper. Possibly a quarter klick out to our northwest," I reported without preamble.

If that sniper had been in position just a minute earlier, both Leora and Logan could have been direct targets. The thought sent a chill through me.

"Setting up on the roof. Ghost, are you hit?" Logan's voice was urgent.

"I'm fine. Keep everyone inside," I responded, trying to keep my voice steady.

"Zar, dammit, are you hit?"

"Gunner, it's just a nick. Relax." I tried to downplay the wound, even as another shot pinged sharply off the barrier right in front of me, forcing me to duck.

Reacting quickly, I stood, fired two retaliatory shots in the direction of the sniper, and then ducked back down. Soon, I heard Logan's footsteps on the roof.

"Ghost, I see him. Permission to neutralize."

"Granted."

A moment later, a single shot rang out, followed by Logan's chuckle through the phone, a sound strangely comforting despite the situation.

"Tango down," he paused, his tone shifting to business. "I'll go check him out with Cipher. Go get some medical attention."

I sighed deeply, the adrenaline beginning to ebb. I waited a moment, gathering myself, then headed back inside to tend to the wound.

Leora

I heard it. Logan's shot. The moment he started to call Zarek when he hadn't come back inside, my gut tightened. And then when I saw him take a sniper gun I couldn't name and head to the roof, I almost lost it.

Zarek finally entered the warehouse. His black t-shirt was bunched up on his right shoulder and he was looking at a large gash on his bicep. Blood trickled down his arm and my breath caught in my throat.

I could've lost him. But he wasn't even mine to lose.

'I'm sorry. In case it's the last thing I say.'

"Amelia!" he bellowed just as she ran to him with a first aid kit.

Kabir was gearing up to head out with Logan and check on the intruder.

"You good, Ghost?" he asked calmly.

Why is he calm? Zarek just got shot!

"Fine. It's just a nick," Zarek replied.

I remained glued to my position near the kitchen. I had been planning to make a sandwich for myself when the commotion started.

Zarek's eyes met mine and his expression morphed from one of irritation to unmistakable concern. He shrugged away Amelia's hand who was cleaning his wound, and strode towards me with an urgency. He cupped my cheeks and ran his thumbs under my eyes. It took me a few seconds to realize that he was wiping away my tears.

Shit. Am I crying?

I blinked away the sudden blurriness and pressed my hands on his chest. He was all muscle and hard beneath my palms.

"I'm fine," he whispered.

I stayed perfectly motionless, not a single muscle twitching.

"Leora, look at me. I'm fine," his voice turned desperate. He seized my mouth with his, pulling me close until there was no space between our bodies. It was a kiss born of pure desperation. An attempt to bring me back from the haze I was in. I couldn't move my lips, didn't kiss him back. I just stood there, paralyzed by the picture of him lying in the sweltering heat behind the warehouse, bleeding out on the grass.

He broke away, his eyes scanning mine.

"Come back to me, baby. *Breathe*. I'm right here. I'm okay."

His words finally put me out of my trance and I jerked to reality. He was fine. Zarek was fine. He wasn't outside, bleeding to death. I cradled his face, seeking the warmth of his skin to assure myself of his presence, and the dam within me burst, releasing sobs that had been coiled tight in my chest. He pulled me against him and rubbed my back.

"Shh, it's alright. I've got you."

After a moment, I gently pushed against Zarek's chest, my voice barely a whisper. "You need to get that wound cleaned properly," I said, my eyes avoiding the raw gash on his arm.

Zarek nodded, a shadow of reluctance in his eyes.

I turned and hurried to my room, closing the door softly. Inside, I leaned against it, my body shaking with silent sobs. I buried my face in my hands, stifling the wails that threatened to escape.

EIGHTEEN

Leora

In the evening, the team gathered around the dining table, glasses in hand, trying to unwind. Logan, noticing my red-rimmed eyes, quipped, "What's the matter, Leo, cat videos again?"

I forced a smile, my eyes briefly meeting Zarek's before darting away.

Logan's expression turned serious. "So, about this morning's excitement—turns out our sniper friend was probably a hired gun. I've handed him over to the authorities."

"Our hideout's compromised, though. We're moving to a new safe house tomorrow." Kabir added.

The room filled with a tense silence, punctuated by the clink of glass as Dylan poured another whiskey.

"Sorry for being useless." He mumbled and chugged his drink down.

"Relax, Dyl. You're useless for another twenty-four hours," Logan smiled at him mockingly and Dylan shoved him with his bad arm, only to wince and laugh.

"I guess I'm driving tomorrow?" Kabir asked, spinning the ice in his drink.

"Yep," Logan patted on his shoulder.

Zarek kept his gaze locked on his glass.

Amelia was at the end of the table, absorbed in her own world. She alternated between tweaking components on her drone and tapping rapidly on her laptop, engrossed in her work.

I sat quietly, my gaze occasionally drifting to Zarek's bandaged arm.

"Do you have a minute?" Zarek asked me hesitantly, just as I was about to pour myself a drink.

"I don't know," Logan grinned, "I'm pretty busy with this whiskey right now, Zarek."

Zarek shook his head and gestured for me to follow him. With a glass in hand, he led the way to his room. Once inside, I snatched the glass from him and downed its contents in one swift gulp, the straight whiskey burning my throat.

"Uh, I was working on that," his eyes met my glare, "but yeah, go ahead. Do you want another one?"

"It's fine," my hoarse voice surprised me. I hadn't spoken since my very long breakdown in my room earlier.

"Leora, I–"

"It's too late, you know." I said blankly, "I'm already that helpless woman. I care about you enough already that I had a panic attack in my room afterward."

"Baby, it happens."

"*'Baby'*. Seriously?" I challenged, arching an

eyebrow at him as he advanced, backing me against his door.

"Do you hate it?" he countered, his presence overwhelming as he closed in, trapping me with nowhere to go.

I scoffed, turning my head to avoid his intense gaze. "Really? After two years, I let my guard down for someone who doesn't even know what he wants."

Zarek lowered his head, his defeat palpable in the slumped set of his shoulders.

When he didn't respond, I continued. "*You* are the one who said *when* not *if*. *You* are the one who fucked me right outside this room. *You*, Zarek."

He didn't even try to defend himself, just sighed. Running a hand through his hair, a tortured look crossed his face.

"I get it, I frustrate you," he murmured. "But you *know* why I hesitate. You know what I'm terrified of."

He met my glare then. "Leora, I—"

"Don't 'Leora' me when you're busy pushing me away one minute and pulling me close the next," I interrupted, my voice sharp.

Zarek exhaled heavily, his frustration mirroring mine. "I'm trying to protect you. Don't you understand that? I'm trying to not get you killed."

I snapped, tired of the same old excuses. "Stop deciding what I can or cannot handle. Maybe I want to be a part of this squad—maybe I want you, despite the risks."

He stared at me, conflict written all over his face, caught between desire and his sense of duty. His hand reached to cup my face but I swatted it away.

His face crumpled as he spoke. "*God*, you keep pulling me in, and " He paused, catching his breath.

"But the thought of anything happening to you... I can't handle that, Leora. *Please*, you can't possibly want this. You can't possibly want *me*."

His voice started softly, almost a plea, but by the end, his words were a crushing blow.

I can't want this? I can't want him?

He seemed to think that joining the squad and being with him are the same thing. Perhaps, they were. They resulted in the same terrifying outcome in his head. That thought kept bouncing around in my head, leaving a dull ache behind.

"When will you realize that I'm already in this too deep? There's no stepping back now. This... all of this will follow me for the rest of my life, Zarek." I whispered back.

He just stared at me, silent, his eyes a tumult of emotions I couldn't decipher. So I pressed on, my voice rising.

"You're very..." I gave him an irritated shrug, "Hot and cold. Unsure. What the fuck do *you* want?"

"Fuck, Leora. I don't know!" He bellowed, "You drive me crazy all the time. When you didn't move and kept crying in front of me, I lost my mind," his hand caressed my throat, "When I saw those marks on your neck, my knees gave out. And when I saw..." his thumb traced my jaw and his eyes darkened, "when I saw Casteel's partner almost rape you, I shot his dick off."

I pushed him back. My eyes widened at his admission.

I was almost what?

"Wha—"

"Tell me, Leora," his voice was gentle yet strained. "What do you think I want, because to me it's clear that I want *you*. But I can't just have you, can I? Because I've told you this a million times. If I really have you, I put you in danger and misery for the rest of your life."

"Let *me* decide that."

"I can't," his head dropped to my shoulder, "I fucking can't, baby. You'll lose me. Or worse, I'll lose you. I can't let that happen. You can't be another picture in my wallet."

"Let *me* decide who I choose to lose. Let *me* decide where I belong," I whispered, my hand resting hesitantly on his back.

That's when I heard him mutter a curse, his head angling toward my neck and he peppered me with soft kisses. I tilted my head to give him more room and felt him smile, his breath hot against my skin.

"You're making me lose my mind," he mumbled between kisses.

"And you love it!" I whispered.

"I do love it, *Mi Corazón.*"

I paused at the new endearment. It was Spanish.

"You're Spaniard, I forgot," my voice was breathless.

He pinned me against the door and lifted me to get a better angle on my neck. My legs instinctively wrapped around his waist and I felt the unmistakable bulge in his sweatpants.

"You don't like me calling you baby, so I had to get creative," he gently pressed his lips to mine. Parting my lips, his tongue tangled with mine with a controlled urgency. When I moaned into his mouth, a guttural groan escaped him.

"Fuck, we're doing this, huh?" He whispered, surrendering. He was finally giving in.

"Yeah, are you scared?" I smiled coyly.

His hands tightly gripped my thighs and slowly slid towards my ass. I was wearing thin silk shorts loose enough for his fingers to easily gain their path to my soaked panties.

"I'm fucking terrified. But know that once we do this, there's no going back, *Mi Corazón*." His breath tickled my cheeks.

I gripped his shoulders tighter. I wasn't sure whether I was afraid to fall, or just fall for him.

When he felt the wetness through the fabric, he pulled back slightly. "God, you're so fucking wet for me, Dr. Leora Mateez."

His lips crashed on mine and he was no longer gentle.

As I came up for air, I mumbled. "Zarek, I need you to–"

"I know what you need, *Mi Corazón*. Let's do it properly this time."

He carried me to his bed and gently laid me down. His body consumed mine as he loomed over me and lapped his mouth on me again. His hands grabbed the hem of my tank top and pulled it up.

Tracing a path from my jaw down to my neck, he found a tender spot between my breasts. Gently, he eased the cup of my bra aside and gazed up at me, his eyes clouded with a yearning that mirrored my own.

"I've been dreaming about taking these into my mouth since that day." He murmured, his voice rough with desire.

His mouth closed over my breast, his tongue teasing my nipple into a taut peak, drawing a soft whimper from deep within me.

"Zarek," I breathed out, my hands weaving into

his hair.

"I've got you," he assured in a whisper, his breath hot against my skin.

The room was thick with silence, punctuated only by the sound of our breaths. His lips, which had been tracing a path down my stomach, paused at the two tiny, reminders of my past—my stab scars. This was something he didn't see that feverish night. His eyes clouded with something dark for a moment, his touch halting.

"Is this from—"

I cut him off, breathless from the heat of the moment, "Zarek, just leave it."

But he wouldn't let it go, not yet. "I can't just ignore these, *Mi Corazón,*" he murmured.

"It all led me to you," I replied softly, trying to bridge the distance his concern had created. "I don't care anymore, Zarek."

He studied my face for a long moment, as if searching for traces of the pain that had once defined these scars. Then, with a tenderness that made my heart swell, he pressed a gentle kiss on each scar, his breath warm against the chill of my skin.

He lingered there, forehead resting against my stomach, a silent vow passing through his touch. He nodded against my belly, and then slowly, he continued his descent, his movements deliberate. With a careful ease, he hooked his fingers around the waistband of both my shorts and panties, peeling them away in a smooth, deliberate motion.

Grasping my thighs, he parted them, his gaze burning with unmistakable hunger that sent another wave of anticipation through me.

He kissed my inner thigh. "All wet for me, Leora,"

his lips touched a bit higher towards my knee.

"Stop teasing me," I moaned.

"Is that so, beautiful?"

Suddenly he dove in, flattening his tongue between my legs and sucked hard. His tongue flicked my swollen clit, and his fingers smeared my wetness over my folds.

Before I could take a breath, his finger slid inside me and hooked, hitting the right spot, and I let out a desperate cry.

"Oh God, Zarek!"

I moaned as quietly as I could while latching on to his hair for dear life, pushing him deeper between my thighs, shamelessly grinding on his face. A chuckle led me to stop, and he lifted my hips to get better access.

"So fucking greedy."

One finger replaced two and my soul lit on fire. He didn't separate his lips from my folds and his tongue continued its feral dance over my clit.

"You taste so good, Leora."

He sucked.

Flicked.

Nibbled.

"I could feast on you all fucking day."

I was so damn close, and Zarek's throaty voice started to undo me.

"Come for me, *Mi Corazón.*"

Pleasure ripped through my bones and heat flooded my cheeks as my orgasm hit me. My vision blurred and came back into focus. I could no longer control my loud moans as I descended through the ecstatic high.

"*Zarek,*" I moaned.

He didn't let go of my clit and let me ride through

the end of my white-hot release until my legs shivered and my bones melted. I clutched his head with my thighs and he finally let go.

He rose, cradled my face in his hand, and kissed me senselessly as I came down from the breathless high.

My hands reached down from his abs to his throbbing cock in his sweatpants, but he stopped me.

"It's not about me today. I rejected you too many times. You need to know I want you, Leora," he kissed me again, "I want you. So," *kiss*, "Damn," *kiss*, "Much." *Kiss*.

His hands snaked my waist and he twisted us, so I was lying nearly on top of him. We remained silent for a good few minutes, and then I decided to break the silence.

"Zarek?"

"Hmm?"

"I want to join the squad."

He sighed and then surprisingly chuckled, "I feel used."

I leaned into his warmth, my laughter fading as I noticed the sudden shift in his expression—a shadow of concern.

"You won't have to go through that kind of hell again, Leora." His voice was firm, threaded with a promise that was as heartfelt as it was impossible. His eyes burned with a determination that both comforted and saddened me.

I managed a small, unsure nod, aware of the complexities of his life. This was something I knew he couldn't promise.

My fingers traced a path along his chest, moving up to a small, rugged scar just above his collarbone.

Before I could ask, he caught the curiosity in my gaze and murmured softly. "Bullet wound, three years ago. We walked into an ambush during what was supposed to be a straightforward rescue op."

I didn't stop there. My fingers, trembling, drifted to another scar near his ribs—a stark, jagged line. "Stab wound, about seven years ago," he continued, a shadow passing over his features. "Logan pulled me out of that mess. Saved me for, I think, the twelfth time before I got stabbed again."

My hands found his recently bandaged arm, and my heart ached at the sight. Noticing my concern, he gave me a reassuring smile. "Just a bullet graze from this morning. It's nothing serious—won't even leave a mark."

As I pressed closer, wrapping my arms around him tightly, comforted by the rise and fall of his steady breathing, he broke the silence again, his voice hesitant. "Would you ever tell me about him?"

As I traced idle circles on his chest, my expression clouded with a frown. "It's not really a story worth telling," I began, my voice tinged with hesitation. "I met him at a cafe. He was charming. But looking back, he was also incredibly pushy."

I paused, lifting my gaze to meet Zarek's. "I really don't remember the worst of it. It's called trauma-induced amnesia. I remember bits and pieces leading up to it, though. He was very controlling. Didn't want me to hang out with Ally. He despised her, actually. Then when I got promoted to Resident Psychologist, I was out more. Getting called in at night. He became very protective. At least that's how I defined it then."

Zarek's embrace tightened, his discomfort palpable

as I continued. "One night, I got home around four in the morning. I was just taking off my shoes when he threw me against the door. The handle dug into my back, and I screamed. He was ranting about smelling men's perfume on me. I couldn't understand a fucking word. Everything was hazy. That's the day the beatings started. Until eventually, one day, he stabbed me with my own kitchen knife and left the apartment."

Zarek's sigh was laden with a restrained fury. "Baby, this is fucked up. Who found you?"

"My mom," I answered quietly. "She dropped by the next day to leave something—I can't even remember what. But yeah... she found me there."

He shook his head, the muscles in his jaw working. To shift the heaviness of our conversation, I added with a half-hearted chuckle, "You know, I had to live with my parents for a year after that? Talk about a different kind of torture."

His eyes softened, and he pulled me closer. "You're the strongest, bravest, most amazing woman I have ever had the privilege to meet, let alone be saved by."

"Privilege to stalk." I corrected, chuckling.

"You know, I wouldn't want to take back that time. I needed every second of it."

I smiled and nestled closer into his embrace. The weight of the past seemed a little lighter with him by my side, and we remained entwined like that until it was time for dinner.

NINETEEN

Zarek

I didn't catch a wink of sleep. Leora was curled up against me, her breath warm on my neck. It should have been comforting, but a restless fear was creeping into my heart. In my gut, I knew we needed to be together to face what was coming.

But there it was—that gnawing fear every time I pictured her with the squad, suited up and in the line of fire. She had chosen this path for herself, boldly stepping into danger, and it wasn't my place to pull her back. I had no right to make this call for her.

So, there I was, wide awake, thinking about how I could possibly make her journey smoother, how I could support her without stepping over the line. I needed to shake off this urge to control, to protect her from everything. If I didn't loosen up, she'd be right to walk away. And I surely wasn't ready for that.

✧ ✧ ✧

The morning came in with a startling commotion. Loading up the cars, I made multiple trips from the rooms to the cars that were now parked inside the warehouse using our sneaky garage door on the side wall. Kabir kept a watch on the camera feed for any new snipers or ambush near us.

I walked past Leora on one of the trips and she gave me a wink. I never thought I'd be blushing over a woman, not at this age. But here I was, heat flooding my cheeks.

"I guess I won't need to bunk in the command center," Kabir grinned.

"Because…?" I gave him a confused look.

"Won't you and Leora be shacking up?" he gave a knowing smirk wiggling his brows.

I shoved a case of magazines to his chest, "Get this in the Escalade."

Once we were all packed and ready, we took off to our new safehouse which was across Toronto, on the other side of Ontario. Passing through the Gardiner Expressway and sliding past the CN tower, I saw Leora looking out the window with a slight sheen in her eyes. It was clear she missed her old life.

"Can we–" she started, "Never mind."

"What is it?" I asked her, peaking through the mirror and glancing at Logan asleep cradling his glock in his hand close to his chest.

"A detour would be dangerous, right?" she asked hesitantly.

I nodded, "It would. Where did you want to go, *Mi Corazón?*"

I heard a faint snort from the back seat. *Fucker.*

"My parents' house. Logan told me they were informed of my absence. But I just wanted to see them myself, you know?"

I sighed. This was how I was going to show that I trusted her to make her own choices. "I guess we could drop you off there. You can meet them for a day, explain your absence, and we'll pick you up tomorrow?"

"What if–"

"Logan can play guard dog."

"Logan can't. But Leo's man can," he mumbled from the backseat.

I rolled my eyes and smiled.

"Are you sure?" Leora asked me, her voice shaky.

I nodded and pressed a button on the dash that connected me with the other car.

"Rivera 32577, confirming detour to Milton," I said.

"Desmond 39901, copy," Amelia's voice came through, "Ghost, why?"

"Leora wants to stay overnight with her parents. I'll watch guard, Logan can drive the rest with you guys."

A faint *"whipped"* sounded on the comms. *Kabir.* Amelia cleared her throat and continued, "Got it, Boss."

I disconnected and looked at Logan through the mirror, "You good to drive?"

He groaned and sat up, "Yep. When should I pick you both up tomorrow?"

"1300 hours," Leora answered before I could respond.

"Oooh, already practicing being Alpha Squad 6, huh?" Logan singsonged.

I saw Leora smile in my peripheral vision.

Thirty minutes later we pulled up near a small suburban house in Milton. The house was well maintained, its brown bricks and white accents gave it a homely yet beautiful look.

As I removed my gear and vest to appear less daunting, Logan slid into the driver's seat and drove away. I noticed Leora exhale shakily before she made her way to the front door. Matching her pace, I caught up and intertwined our fingers.

She pressed the doorbell, and shortly after, a white-haired woman swung the door open. The shock and joy on her face were palpable as she pulled Leora into a tight embrace, tears brimming in her eyes immediately. "Ora, my baby," she exclaimed, holding her close.

Behind her, an older man—Leora's father—appeared, his face breaking into a relieved smile. Oliver and Alessandra Mateez, both doctors at UHN, radiated warmth and concern. The depth of their greeting struck me, contrasting sharply with the distant relationship I had with my own parents, who hadn't bothered to look for me during my years of no-contact. I knew if Zavier was still alive, I'd be granted my warm familial greeting. But that was no longer an option.

"Are you hurt?" Oliver's voice was laced with concern as he gently cupped Leora's cheeks.

Shaking her head, Leora reassured, "I'm completely fine."

Their attention then shifted to me. With a slightly nervous smile, Leora introduced me, "This is Detective Zarek Rivera. He's a cop I'm working with."

My surprise must have flickered across my face, but I quickly masked it. What was she playing at?

Before I could utter a word of greeting, Leora quickly suggested, "Let's go inside. I'll explain everything there."

We settled into their cozy living room, taking a seat on the gray couch. Her parents sat across from us, their eyes curious and a bit cautious.

"Are you two dating?" Oliver didn't waste a moment.

"Dad!" Leora's protest echoed around the room.

I extended my hand. "Hello, Dr. and Mrs. Mateez. It's lovely to meet you both. I apologize for not introducing myself properly earlier," I said, raising an eyebrow playfully at Leora.

Oliver's handshake was firm, betraying his need for reassurance about the man with his daughter.

Alessandra, ever the hopeful, chimed in with a gentle smile, "So, you two *are* dating?"

"We're new, ma'am," I admitted, a soft smile playing on my lips.

"Oh, please. Call me Sandra," she smiled back and turned to Leora, "He's very handsome, Ora."

"Mom," Leora glared at her.

I gave Leora a soft kiss on her temple and whispered, "I'll step out so you can talk, okay?" She gave a small nod, and I walked towards the sliding glass door that led to the backyard.

About fifteen minutes later, Oliver joined me, carrying two glasses. He handed me one filled with whiskey and ice. "Thank you, Dr. Mateez."

"Please, call me Oliver," he insisted with a dismissive wave of his hand. He then took a moment to study my face intently before speaking. "She told us about the risks she's facing. Thank you for being there for her, Zarek."

"It's part of the job," I replied respectfully.

"Were you in the military?" he asked, catching me slightly off guard.

I nodded, managing a small smile. "Yes, sir, I was."

"And now a detective?"

I paused, wary of the discrepancy between what Leora might have told him and my actual story. "I—"

"You're not really a detective, are you?" His expression turned steely.

"Dr. Mateez—"

He set both our glasses down on the patio table with a firm clink and fixed me with a scrutinizing gaze. My heart raced, wondering if I'd been found out.

"Zarek Rivera," he mused under his breath, then looked up sharply. "I know a special unit man when I see one."

I froze.

He extended his hand again, and as I reached out, he yanked me closer. "Major Oliver Mateez, ex-CSIS, military doctor," he disclosed in a low tone, his eyes piercing. "Does Leora know the truth about you?"

I nodded, the revelation of his past and identity sending a chill through me. "She knows, sir. She wasn't fooled. But what about you? Does she know about your past?"

He chuckled softly, "I'm no longer that person, Zarek. I met Alessandra after a mission went bad. In a few weeks I quit the force. Retired to be a normal, boring old doctor," he smiled.

I smiled back at him, but quickly a shadow took over my expression. I wasn't planning on quitting

Alpha Squad. Did her father expect a normal life for her, a life she would never get with me? White picket fence, brick house in the suburbs.

I can't give her that.

I was about to speak when Leora stepped out into the sunlight, her skin shining golden in the sunlight. Her appearance momentarily distracted me, and I lost my train of thought.

"Mom is calling us for lunch."

Oliver gave a nod and picked up his whiskey, heading back inside. I pulled her closer, stealing a quick, tender kiss that seemed to lighten her spirits as a small smile graced her lips.

"What was that for?" she murmured, her eyes searching mine for clues.

"Just needed to catch my breath for a moment," I confessed, allowing a broad grin to spread across my face.

"Aren't we already outside?" she teased, her chuckle mingling with the evening breeze.

I responded by kissing the tip of her nose, a playful shrug accompanying my gesture. "Just making sure you're really here," I joked.

She leaned into me, her voice lowering as she shared, "My parents told Ally and the others I'm okay. They were freaking out when I disappeared on my birthday."

"Should we meet up with them, maybe reassure them in person?" I suggested, half-hoping to integrate more normalcy into the chaos that had become her life.

She shook her head firmly. "It's better if they stay out of this. I don't want anyone else getting dragged into this mess."

My lips twitched into a half-smile at her protective instinct. "So you're saying you'd want to keep them safe from this life, huh?" I teased, echoing her earlier concerns about involvement.

She caught the irony immediately and gave me a playful shove. "Zarek Rivera, you do *not* get to turn my words around on me. They're not in this, not like I am."

I chuckled, accepting my defeat, but my gaze couldn't help wandering over the serene backyard setting. Turning back to her, a more serious tone took over. "Do you wish for this?"

"Wish for what?"

"Brick houses, backyards with patio furniture... this?"

She paused, considering the question seriously before letting out a soft sigh. "Are you worried that you might not be able to give me the life you *think* I want?"

I gazed deeply into her eyes, looking for any trace of doubt or hesitation. Finding none, I listened intently.

"I don't want any of this, Zarek. I want *you* and I hope I *have* you."

I kissed her temple and sighed a breath of relief. For now, I would believe her. I spent too much time assuming and deciding for her. No more.

"You have me, *Mi Corazón.*"

But for how long?

TWENTY

Leora

As soon as we pulled up to the new safe house near Woodstock, I slid out of the car, eager to stretch my legs. The warehouse, a behemoth structure, loomed larger and more fortified than our last hideout. Its walls, thick, promised better security, and the discreet underground parking meant our presence would be virtually undetectable from the outside.

This time, Zarek and I shared a room, which, despite its small closet, didn't bother me—I hadn't brought much with me. Amelia had claimed the only other room with an ensuite bathroom, leaving Logan, Kabir, and Dylan to manage with a communal bathroom.

"I really don't give a shit," Kabir declared nonchalantly. "I don't need much space unlike Logan who uses five different hair products."

We were all sitting circling the table in the main

area.

"I do *not*!" Logan retorted.

"Yeah, well, I'm keeping my stuff in my room," Dylan chimed in casually, steering clear of the bathroom debate.

Logan, not one to let the jibe at him slide, raised a hand in protest. "For the record, I use one shampoo, one conditioner, and one hair mask—that's it!"

"That's two more than I use," Kabir quipped, unfazed. "You're not taking the small ass shelf space!"

"Imbecile," Dylan muttered under his breath.

Zarek, Amelia, and I watched the banter unfold with amused smiles, barely suppressing our laughter.

Logan continued to defend his hair care routine with passion. "That's because I care about my hair. Do you know what the constant use of balaclavas can do to your hair?"

"Should we start a support group? 'Balaclavas Anonymous' for affected hair?" Kabir's sarcasm met with a glare from Logan.

Dylan jumped in with a grin. "Maybe Logan should launch his own line of 'Balaclava Safe' hair products. Could be a hit?"

Logan shot Dylan a look that was part annoyance, part amusement. "Hilarious. Remind me to leave you out of my billion-dollar haircare empire."

Kabir laughed, patting Logan on the back. "Don't worry, brother, we'll just be your before photos."

Logan rolled his eyes but couldn't suppress a smile. "Keep it up, and I'll start hiding your gear in shampoo bottles."

Dylan smirked, folding his arms across his chest. "Good luck squeezing my rifle into a conditioner bottle."

"That's a challenge," Logan retorted with a playful nod. "But I bet I could fit Kabir's entire tech setup in my hair mask jar."

Kabir feigned shock, touching his chest in mock horror. "Not the sacred hair mask jar!"

The laughter grew louder, echoing around the sparsely furnished room, and even Zarek shook his head with a chuckle.

The banter slowly wound down as Zarek and I began to unpack, but the lightness it brought remained.

Zarek and I headed to our bedroom.

Our bedroom.

I hadn't originally planned to share a space with Zarek, but now that it was a reality, the idea of being apart from him seemed unimaginable.

As we settled into our new temporary room, Zarek produced a phone from his pocket, extending it toward me with a serious look. "This is yours now. It's secure, but try to keep contact with family and friends to a minimum."

Grasping the phone eagerly, a surge of relief washed over me—it had been days since I'd felt the comforting weight of a phone in my hand. "I need to check my damn email," I half-joked, half-serious. "I'm probably fired by now."

Zarek's response was a soft, amused smile as he watched me power it on and dive into my inbox. My fingers flew over the screen, logging into my mail app, where a flood of unread messages awaited. But it was one particular email that caught my eye—an email from the day after my birthday.

As I scanned the contents, my eyes widened in disbelief. "Zarek, what did you do?" I looked up at him, baffled.

He just shrugged, an enigmatic smirk playing on his lips. "Nothing too obvious. Just keeping your options open."

The email revealed that I had been officially recruited by the Toronto Police Department for a 'special assignment'. Astonishingly, I was still on Detention Center's payroll, a clever maneuver on his part to give me cover and financial security while I navigated this chaos.

This meant I wasn't just away; I was still officially employed, tethered to my old life by a thread he had spun silently behind the scenes. Only until I was ready to go back. And I realized that I might not ever be ready to go back.

✧ ✧ ✧

Dinner wrapped up, but our minds were far from at ease, buzzing back into mission mode. The uncertainty about Jerome Tyson and his notorious father, Garret, kept us plotting non-stop, keen on intercepting their Crazon shipments. The stakes were high; in the wrong hands, Crazon could wreak havoc, a risk we couldn't afford.

As Logan outlined my training schedule post-dinner, debates heated within the squad. "There's no point," Kabir was saying, frustration clear as day, "If we can't fully understand what Crazon is capable of, we're essentially fighting blind, Zarek. We can't know everything with the testing we've been doing."

"I'm not saying we abandon the idea of exploring its capabilities," Zarek said, flipping a Crazon device onto the table, watching it spin aimlessly. "Let's just hold off until we get the green light from above. The intrusive tests are not authorized, yet."

Amelia shook her head in disagreement, and Dylan, ever the stoic, said nothing. Logan kept out of it, leaving Kabir and Zarek locked in a typical showdown. "And I'm arguing for immediate action. They'll give us the nod, I'm sure of it," Kabir countered and Zarek shook his head.

"I think," I interjected hesitantly. "We can't afford to wait. What if our delay puts the entire squad at risk? We hardly know anything about it. What if it puts us a step behind?"

Kabir gestured supportively towards me then crossed his arms, a smug look plastered across his face. Zarek's eyes narrowed, his irritation palpable. "So you think they're already outmaneuvering us?"

"The longer we wait, the more advantage we give them. If we don't know what can hurt us, it inevitably will," I pressed on, my resolve hardening.

"And what? Following protocol is now pointless?" Zarek's voice was sharp, slicing through the tension.

"I'm saying endless debating might be costing us while they could be actively using this device against us," I shot back, locking eyes with him, my voice rising.

Zarek exhaled sharply, frustration etched across his face. "Fine," he conceded begrudgingly, his glance flicking towards Kabir, "Go ahead, do it."

He stormed off towards our bedroom, his stride stiff with annoyance. Kabir shot me a victorious thumbs up. I rolled my eyes and followed my very annoyed Zarek to our room.

As I entered our room, I found Zarek in a storm

of frustration, swiftly peeling off his t-shirt and stepping out of his sweatpants. He snatched a towel and headed straight for the bathroom. My mind was set; I was going to join him, hopefully easing some of that tension that the earlier debate had wound into his muscles.

But the moment I stepped into the bathroom after stripping my clothes off, his eyes met mine—not with softness but with a hardened, fiery glare. "You think you can defy me in front of everyone?" he growled, his voice rough with barely contained anger.

A smirk tugged at my lips, amused by his almost petulant tone. "I can voice my opinions, can't I?" I challenged, meeting his intensity head-on.

He grunted and shed his boxers. I expected anger, but the way his hard cock sprang free and his eyes devoured my naked form suggested a different kind of frustration.

"Enter the shower," he commanded, a steely note in his voice. I complied, stepping under the warm spray. Instantly, his hands gripped my waist, spinning me to face away from him. The water cascaded down on us.

Smack.

A sharp whimper escaped me as his hand connected firmly with my ass. "Undermining me in front of my squad is going to cost you."

The unexpected sting sent a jolt through me.

"Now, *Mi Corazón,*" he murmured, his hand soothing the spot he had just struck.

Smack.

"We will have to do something about your defiance," he declared, a thrilling edge to his voice, as I reveled in the delicious mix of pain and pleasure.

"And what will that be?" I asked, my tone thick with arousal, turning slightly to look over my shoulder.

His lips hovered near my ear, his breath hot against my skin. Even with the shower's roar, his whisper cut through. "I'm going to make you scream louder than you fucking argued."

Abruptly, his fingers plunged into my slick heat, thrusting deep and drawing a fervent moan from my lips.

"So fucking wet for me, huh?" He growled into the steamy air of the shower.

"You got all worked up just by arguing with me?" He asked, his question rhetorical.

His fingers moved rhythmically inside me, coaxing louder moans with each stroke.

"Baby, *please*." I pleaded him to go faster, do more, do anything.

His other hand wrapped around my waist, his thumb pressing hard on my clit, eliciting a raw, guttural cry from the depths of my throat.

He expertly manipulated my clit, fingers still curling inside me, relentlessly seeking that perfect spot. My head fell forward, resting against the cool tile wall as a wave of intense pleasure crashed over me, spurred on by another sharp pinch to my sensitive nub.

My legs trembled and gave out, but Zarek was quick to catch me, his arms wrapping around me to steady my shaking body. He turned me in his embrace and carried me from the shower's embrace, the cool air of the bedroom hitting my damp skin.

He laid me down gently on the bed, my wet body imprinting the sheets, as he hovered over me. He flipped me onto my stomach, positioning my legs wide apart as though I were a feast laid out solely for him.

Deliberately, achingly slow, he pressed his tongue against my folds, savoring the taste of my arousal. I quivered, still tingling from the aftershocks of my earlier climax.

Glancing back, I caught his gaze—tender yet intensely passionate. He swept my damp hair aside, planting tender kisses down the length of my spine.

Then, capturing both my wrists, he pinned them behind my back and surged inside me with a single, masterful stroke. A sharp cry escaped me at the exquisite fullness, my breaths coming in short, ragged pulls.

"Bite the pillow. I'm not holding back," he growled deeply.

His thrusts were powerful and deep, sending me teetering on the edge. I craved more—more of him, every part of him.

"Harder, Zarek," I gasped between moans, and his slow, deliberate thrusts transformed into rapid, forceful drives. Zarek lost himself in the fervor, his movements wild with desperation.

"Please, please, please, please, please," I begged for more.

I bit down on the pillow as instructed. My moans—loud enough for the whole squad to hear—muffled slightly.

"Fuck, I love it when you beg." Zarek's voice was breathy. With one final thrust, I was catapulted over the edge, spiraling into a continuous climax. Zarek didn't stop, his rhythm growing even more frenzied. My body shook, every nerve alight with exquisite pleasure, my bones seemingly dissolving in the heat. I was writhing, shivering, twisting in pleasure.

"Zarek," I moaned out his name as waves of endless release swept through me.

With a final deep thrust, he stilled, his groan vibrating through the air as he reached his own climax. He collapsed onto me, his breath cooling the skin of my back.

"Fuck," he exhaled softly, pulling out and then drawing me back against his chest, enveloping me.

"I guess I should argue more," I breathed, a spontaneous giggle bubbling up between us. Zarek's laughter mingled with mine as he began tracing a path of kisses along my neck and up to my jaw. He propped himself on one elbow, gently turning my face towards his. With a look full of deep affection and longing, he paused for a moment before his lips urgently met mine.

TWENTY-ONE

Leora

ONE MONTH LATER

"Did you get it done?" I asked Kabir.

"Yeah, the rent's all paid up, and they cleaned your apartment a couple of days ago," he replied, giving me a quick smile before his expression turned serious. "You haven't told Zarek about keeping your apartment, have you?"

I let out a sigh, feeling the weight of the secret. "No, I just... I need to keep some things separate, for now."

Kabir leaned back in his chair, eyeing me closely. "Zarek told me to terminate your lease and move everything to storage."

A pang of guilt hit me, and I looked down,

wrestling with my attachment to my past life. This relationship with Zarek was still so new, and what if he decided it was too much? Or that he was compromised and a liability to his squad? He had said it once and I didn't fully forget that.

"Just… keep this between us a little longer. I'll tell him, I promise," I said, meeting his gaze.

Kabir shrugged noncommittally, and I headed back out to the main area of the warehouse where we'd been stationed for the past month. My training had been intense, and I felt stronger than ever.

"Finally!" Logan grumbled, "I have been waiting for three minutes."

"Are you really complaining over three minutes, Lo?"

"Punctuality is what I admire in a person. Be on time when I call you next time."

"As you say, Master Lo," I bowed to him dramatically and he gave me a mocking smile.

Logan had been tense since the last mission, which had been a setup—they lost a nonexistent shipment in an ambush. And to top it off, he'd lost his favorite Glock in the chaos, which didn't help his mood.

"I don't have much time before we have to leave for the next assignment," he mumbled.

"I got you, Lo. What do you need?"

"I've set up moving targets thirty yards away. It's a basic multi-position shooting drill. Here are your magz," he handed me a bunch of magazines that I secured in my vest, "Get ready on the whistle."

I nodded, took position, and he whistled.

Once my practice was executed, he ran the score on the target sheets and walked back to me with a tense expression. My heart dropped. My last score had been near perfect, 17 over 20. Did I do worse?

"19 over 20, Leora," he said with a blank expression and handed me the sheets.

"You called me Leora," I said, looking over the sheets.

"That's your name, isn't it?"

"You call me Leo, *Logan.*"

His lips parted to say something but he shut his mouth quickly, "Give me five sets of back squats. You're slow on transition."

"I got 19 over 20," I looked at him, bewildered.

"Five sets. Now."

I went back inside, chalked up my hands, found the barbel, and started my sets. Logan walked past me and sat beside Kabir.

"This Crazon is hard to dispose of," Kabir muttered, "How many were you able to destroy?"

"Seventeen," Logan replied, "Eight are still left."

"And there's a shipment of eight more coming in today. Why eight?"

"Maybe they are an order. Like frickin' Amazon."

Kabir gave him a funny look and sighed.

"We got this, Cipher," Logan patted his back and glanced at me.

Exhausted, I barely finished my third set of squats. My muscles screamed, and a dizzying wave of fatigue washed over me. I'd skipped meals, a mistake given my period had drained my energy even further. But I wasn't about to share that with Logan—dubbed 'Master Lo' today. Gritting my teeth, I initiated another squat, but a sharp cramp clenched my abdomen, sending me collapsing onto the mat. The barbell clanged against the floor, echoing through the room.

Logan shot me a look of sheer irritation and turned away sharply. His mood had soured lately, and I wasn't accustomed to his brooding silence. Feeling a telltale warmth, I rushed to my room, my thoughts a whirl of frustration and discomfort. After changing and downing an Advil, I returned, determined to finish what I'd started.

The barbell was already reset, and Logan stood there, arms crossed, his glare sharp enough to cut. "You do *not* leave the station until I tell you to," he snapped, his voice harsh and unfamiliar.

"Lo, what the hell? I needed the bathroom for a second."

"What the fuck is going on?" Zarek's voice interrupted. He had been cleaning his gun and taking inventory of magz.

"Tell your woman that when I'm in charge of training her, she should listen to every word I say," Logan shouted at Zarek.

"Your problem is with me, Gunner. Don't take it out on her."

"Wait, what problem?" I asked, confused.

Zarek and Logan glared at each other for a good minute and then stormed off in opposite directions. Something was clearly wrong. I saw Kabir shaking his head and slamming his laptop shut. What the fuck was I missing?

I walked to Kabir and sat down next to him.

"You're telling me what that was about."

"Why, the pillow talk didn't bring it up?" he smiled.

My expression remained steady and Kabir sighed.

"During the last mission, Zarek cut the mission short because an alarm went off here. It wasn't a breach or anything but Zarek was adamant that you were in danger. Hell, I checked the cams and showed him that you were dancing around in the kitchen. But he commanded the squad to scale back and leave the shipment. Well, it was a decoy shipment anyway so I didn't care. But Logan clearly thinks Zarek was compromised."

Compromised.

Fuck!

There it was. The word I dreaded. I didn't even remember any alarms going off during their previous assignment.

Kabir's laptop pinged at the same time and he opened it to see a message from his contact.

"The shipment schedule's changed," Zarek announced with a frown, rising swiftly from his seat. "Everyone, assemble. Now!"

Within seconds, the entire squad was on their feet and ready.

"The shipment's been moved up from 1700 to 1400 hours. We have one hour to reach the location," Kabir briefed sharply.

"Squad Six, report for interception sequence and gear up," Zarek commanded, his voice filling the room with urgency.

As they went through their routine of confirming their readiness and loading up the Escalade, I noticed Logan casting wary glances at Zarek, the tension palpable. They needed to resolve whatever was bothering them.

"I want to come with you," I found myself saying to Zarek.

Out of the blue, Logan interjected, "You're not fucking ready, Leora. Stay here." He didn't wait for a response, just turned and walked away.

Zarek's eyes followed him, dark with irritation.

"Hey," I reached up, cupping Zarek's face to draw his gaze back to me. "If he says I'm not ready, then I'm not ready."

He managed a small, strained smile and leaned down to kiss me—a desperate, deep kiss that spoke of a hunger only barely contained.

"I'll be back for more, *Mi Corazón,*" he murmured after breaking the kiss.

With a reluctant nod, he turned and joined the rest of the squad gearing up. I watched them with a tight chest, my anxiety climbing. Before they departed, I approached Logan, wrapping my arms around him from behind.

"Be safe, Lo."

He tensed under my touch, his body rigid.

"Yeah," he murmured hoarsely, breaking from my hold to follow the others.

I stepped back and watched them drive away. Each departure felt just as difficult as the last, and I silently prayed for their safe return.

✧ ✧ ✧

A searing pain on my arm woke me up from my afternoon nap. The squad was gone and I was still struggling with the period pain, so I had decided to nap at the odd hour.

My vision blurred as I blinked awake, sharpening slowly to focus on a figure looming over me. A sharp sting on my arm drew my gaze downward—blood was seeping from a fresh cut, trickling down my skin.

My panic remained in my head while my body

struggled to follow suit. I couldn't move, couldn't scream. My blood leaked through forming a pool near the bed, while another man ran his gloved hands through it, staging a scene for struggle.

"Careful Romano, don't kill her from blood loss," the gloved man laughed.

"Yeah yeah. Are the cams still down? Crazon is amazing at that."

"Yep, we're a go. Jerome moving that shipment was a clever idea, Casteel."

"I'm not forgiving this Zarek guy. He killed Calzone, Mason. I'll fucking end this squad. Jer is tired of them too. Fucking puppets."

Mason chuckled, "Alright. By the way, are we not taking the Crazon they stole from us?"

"We'll get it after," Casteel said, sounding awfully confident, "Hell, we can have this whole fucking warehouse. All their fancy weapons."

"Let's end them, Cas."

Fuck. I was being taken. This was all a trap to eliminate the squad.

They hoisted my paralyzed form effortlessly, carrying me away as darkness crept in from the edges of my vision. Soon, everything went dark.

TWENTY-TWO

Zarek

"Are we good?" I asked Logan as we walked back to our escalade with the shipment. The mission had been pretty easy. Too easy. I shook away the thoughts of Leora being in danger yet again. No alarm went off, everything went smoothly, and the squad was unharmed. Logan had been right. I was compromised for the last mission.

"We're fine. As long as you realize you were being uncharacteristically paranoid," Logan smiled.

"Thanks for saving my ass back there," I said.

"That's twenty, Ghost."

"I'll do anything for you to stop counting," I shook my head and Kabir glanced at us in confusion.

"Counting what?" he asked.

"Nothing," both Logan and I muttered at the same time, although his tone was heaps lighter than my scowling one.

Dylan, overhearing us as he loaded the last of the shipment into the car, couldn't suppress a grin. I fought the urge to roll my eyes at his amusement.

"Men," I heard a faint huff from Amelia.

The squad poured into the Escalade and we drove back to the warehouse. An hour later I was ready to walk back in with Leora waiting at the door ready to jump in my arms as she always did.

But the jump never came.

Maybe she's resting, I thought, considering she hadn't been feeling well. While the rest of the squad secured the shipment and shed their gear, I went straight to our bedroom. Leora was nowhere to be found, and panic set in as my heart raced.

Something is wrong.

I flicked on the lights. My eyes dropped to the floor, and my breath caught. A large pool of blood was smeared across the floor near our bed. My knees buckled, and I collapsed to the ground.

"Logan!" I yelled, my voice cracking as the room spun around me. I heard footsteps rush in, but my stomach churned violently, bile rising up my throat. I vomited.

Leora was gone, hurt, or worse. I was losing it, and I didn't care how weak I looked, vomiting again, powerless and terrified. This is what I was afraid of. Losing her.

This was really happening.

"Zar," Logan's hand landed heavily on my shoulder, his voice a mix of panic and sorrow.

I barely heard him as he spoke. Kabir was setting up his laptop on the bed, Amelia was examining the room with clinical precision, and Dylan was trying to hold Logan together.

"No alarms were triggered, nothing else was missing," Kabir reported, frowning at his screen. "The security cams were offline for 43 minutes this evening."

Logan was pinching the bridge of his nose, trying to stave off a breakdown. "Fuck. Fuck. Fuck!"

"Could it be Casteel again?" I managed to ask, struggling to breathe.

"This blood…" Amelia interrupted, looking closely at the pattern on the floor. "It's too deliberate. There's no blood trail on the bed or out the door. It looks staged."

My head spun with her words, and rage mixed with fear as I shouted, "Stop saying blood!"

Amelia placed a reassuring hand on my shoulder. "Listen, this could mean it's not her blood, or it was taken in a controlled setting. She's likely still alive. I'm 99% sure."

"99%?" Logan's voice thundered with a mix of hope and fear.

"She has to be alive," he added, his voice cracking.

"Logan, she's trained for this. She'll hold on," Dylan tried to reassure him.

Seeing Logan so shaken was surreal; Leora meant as much to him as she did to me. I closed my eyes, trying to block out the sight of the blood, the room spinning around me.

"Find her, Kabir," I rasped out.

"Already on it, Ghost!" Kabir called back, already typing furiously.

✧ ✧ ✧

After splashing water on my face, I stepped back

into the dim hallway of the safehouse, pausing outside my room. The murmur of hushed conversations trickled from the common area. Leaning against the cool doorframe, I caught snippets of Logan's strained voice drifting through the air.

"You don't understand, Dyl. She told me to stay safe, and I just shut her out," Logan said, his voice tinged with regret and something else—fear, maybe.

"Logan, pull yourself together. If you keep this up, Zarek's going to lose it," Dylan replied in a low, steady tone meant to ground his friend.

They hadn't noticed me yet, too caught up in their own world of worry. But Amelia, ever observant, caught my eye from across the room. She offered a small, reassuring smile and subtly signaled to the others. They turned, and the change in Logan's expression was immediate, marked by a mix of surprise and guilt.

"Zar, I'm so—" Logan started, his voice faltering.

I raised a hand, cutting him off. "Don't. You'll apologize to her, not me. And Dylan's right, you know how I'll react if I think you're stepping out of line."

"I don't have feelings for her, Zar. She's like my little sister," Logan quickly clarified, almost defensively.

As he buried his face in his hands, my chest tightened. This wasn't just about keeping the team in line; it was about her—Leora. My fear of losing her gnawed at me, a relentless reminder of what was at stake.

Turning to Kabir, I tried to keep my voice even. "Got anything, Kabir?"

Kabir's eyes were laser-focused on his laptop, his fingers paused above the keyboard. After a tense moment, his face hardened with resolve. "I've tracked a black SUV and a red Tesla Roadster swapping passengers at a gas station about twenty-five kilometers from here. The SUV came back empty, and the Tesla headed to a nondescript house in Stratford."

My heart skipped a beat. Stratford. It could be a break or another dead end, but we had to move fast. Nodding decisively, I felt the leader in me take over, pushing down the personal terror that threatened to overwhelm me.

"Squad Six, gear up. We're heading to Stratford," I commanded, my voice steady despite the storm of dread inside. "This is a rescue mission, and we're bringing her back."

The room sprang into action, the weight of the situation settling over us like a dense fog. As they prepared, I pulled on my tactical vest, each click of the clasps a reminder of what was on the line. Not just a mission. Not just a teammate. But my *Leora*. I realized it then. No matter what, she was ingrained into me. I couldn't let her go.

TWENTY-THREE

Leora

The faint scent of leather hit me as I came to, my hands bound tightly behind my back.

Damn it.

Memories of the afternoon trickled back in a disorienting rush—I had been snatched from the safehouse. Peering through half-lidded eyes, I could see the blur of streetlights zipping past. It was dark outside; how long had I been unconscious?

My arm was wrapped in a bloody bandage, marking the spot where they must have cut me. "She's awake, Cas," Mason's voice cut through the silence.

I shifted my weight and managed to sit up.

"Leora, Leora, Leora," Casteel's voice was taunting. "How are you feeling, little bird?"

"Long time no see, Casteel. How's your friend's dick?" I coughed out a laugh, which earned me a furious glance.

His grip whitened on the steering wheel. "You fucking bitch."

"Mind telling me where we're headed?" I asked, trying to gauge our destination.

He glanced back briefly. "Why, so you can signal your boyfriend? Don't worry, we're counting on him showing up."

Moments later, we pulled up to a row house in what looked like a suburban development. Most of the houses here were still under construction. Roughly, Casteel yanked me from the car and pushed me towards the house.

Inside, the darkness was almost complete, broken only by the outline of three large trunks against the walls. They dragged me upstairs to a room with a single chair in the center.

"Deja vu," I remarked, eyeing the chair.

"How are you still talking? We drained like a pint of your blood," Mason scoffed.

"Shut up, Leora. Another word, and we won't bother stopping the bleeding next time we cut you," Casteel threatened, looming inches from my face.

I walked over to the chair and sat down without them needing to force me. They didn't bother with further restraints. Little did these idiots know, I had been training to escape from zip ties. Over a month of preparation was about to pay off. I had to get out of here before my squad risked their lives coming for me.

Fuck. My squad.

They shut me in the room, and I quickly assessed my surroundings. Other than the chair I had been sitting on, the only other piece of furniture was a single trunk under the window, much like the ones I'd seen outside. It seemed deliberately placed for me to notice. I nudged it open with my feet.

Inside, I recoiled in shock. A digital screen was attached to what looked unmistakably like a bomb. They planned to blow us all up.

Crouching down, I managed to get my bound hands from behind me to the front by looping my feet through the ties. With a sharp pull, I snapped the zip ties and freed myself, ignoring the pain that shot through my wrists.

The window above the trunk was barred from the outside. The door, I assumed, was locked.

I needed a plan, fast.

Shaking off my disbelief, I tried the door handle. It turned easily. It was unlocked.

What the hell?

Descending the stairs, I found the house eerily silent and empty—no sign of Casteel or Mason. The back door and all windows were boarded up. The three trunks downstairs were also packed with explosives.

Rushing to the front door, I discovered it was securely locked. A wire extended from the lock, connected to another digital display.

It hit me then—this was a trap. Once my squad arrived and forced the door, the entire place would explode. The plan was messy, sure to require extensive cleanup.

Suddenly, a car screeched outside, followed by the ominous beeping of the trunks. I darted back to one and saw the countdown on its screen: 4 minutes, 51 seconds... 4 minutes, 50 seconds. *Fuck.*

The squad was here.

Panic surged as sweat beaded my forehead. My

strength was sapped from the day's ordeals—no food, significant blood loss. Even if I got out, they might still detonate the bombs.

Then, a loud bang on the main door.

I sprinted towards it.

"Zarek?" I yelled out.

"Leora?" His voice was muffled through the door. "Step back, I'm going to break it down."

"No, no! Stop!" I screamed as he began to pound on the door. "There are explosives everywhere in here. Casteel's set us up to blow. I need to find another way out or...*fuck*."

I heard him curse from the other side.

"Is there a timer?" he asked urgently.

"Yes, about four minutes left now."

"Leora, I need to get you out. Let me break the door," he pleaded, his voice filled with desperation.

"No, Zarek! If you break the door, the house will explode. Please, just back away," I begged, tears streaming down my face.

"Leo, are you saying you can't use this door at all?" Logan's voice joined in.

"Exactly," I replied. "There's a device linked to the lock. If the lock breaks, the house goes up. You all need to get out now!"

"I'm not leaving without you, *Mi Corazón*," Zarek's voice broke.

I couldn't let this be the end for us. "Get back to the car!" I shouted as loud as I could and made my way upstairs.

I had to find another way out. Maybe there was an attic. Running through the upper floor, I desperately searched for any sign of an attic entrance.

There it was—a square panel on the ceiling.

I pulled down the attic ladder, climbed up quickly, and let my eyes adjust to the dim light. Moonlight filtered through a dusty skylight at the back of the attic. I crawled toward it, heart pounding, and managed to open it.

I clambered out onto the roof, but just as I tried to climb down, the ground suddenly wasn't beneath my feet anymore.

An explosion thundered behind me, hurling me into the air. I felt myself falling, a sharp pain rocketing through my head as the ground rushed up to meet me.

My vision blurred, and then, everything went dark.

TWENTY-FOUR

Zarek

No, no, NO!

She was on the roof, edging out of the attic just as the world below her erupted. The explosion—a roar in my ears, a blinding flash in my eyes. And then, nothing. She disappeared into the chaos. My squad held me back, their hands heavy on my shoulders, but I couldn't contain the grief that tore through me, my name for her dissolving into a scream lost in the fire.

Her voice haunted me, her last words urging us to get to safety, to leave her behind.

"I'm going to check the backyard. Stay here, Zarek."

As soon as Logan's words registered, I bolted.

Ignoring Logan's shouts, I ran, the adrenaline a bitter surge in my veins. I leaped over the fence into the next yard, landing amidst a scene of devastation—bricks and broken wood scattered like the aftermath of a storm, flames greedily claiming what was left.

The squad was right behind me, but their words were distant, muffled by the drum of my heart. "We'll search too," someone said, but I was already moving, driven by a single, terrifying need.

Then, through the smoke and fire, a figure—her figure—emerged. Disappearing and reappearing like a ghost, she rolled on the ground, smothering the flames that licked at her clothes.

Leora.

Her face was streaked with soot, blood seeping from a cut on her forehead, but when our eyes met, she offered a weak, pained smile.

I was at her side in seconds, pulling her into an embrace that was both a relief and a reaffirmation of my deepest fears. "You're alive," I gasped, tears mingling with the ash on my face.

"I'm okay, Zarek," she whispered back, her voice faint.

But then her strength failed her; her body grew heavy against mine. Her arms drooped, lifeless, her head lolled back, and I caught her just before she could hit the ground. A cold dread replaced the heat of the fire.

Cradling her in my arms, I carried her, the squad behind us as we made our way back to the safety of our car.

✧ ✧ ✧

She sat up too quickly for me to react. We were still in the car, heading back to the safehouse.

"Clear," Kabir announced, checking the area from

the front seat.

Leora was between Logan and me in the back, her head had been resting in my lap, but now she was upright, frantically looking around.

"Leo, focus on me," Logan said, gripping her shoulders. "It's me, Logan. You're safe. We're on our way back."

She straightened up, her voice barely above a whisper, "Did anyone from the squad get hurt?"

"No one's hurt, baby. We're all here," I reassured her, pulling her into my arms. Her hands brushed against my face, her expression softening.

"Good. Because I'm about to finish Casteel off, and I'll need some help from the squad," she said, a steely determination in her smile.

"We've got your six," I smiled back and kissed her.

Logan chuckled deeply. "Taught you well, didn't I?"

Leora shot him a blank look, and he visibly winced. It was clear there was some tension between them.

We arrived at the safehouse soon after. I carried Leora inside, hoping she wouldn't notice the still-uncleaned blood and vomit. I gently laid her on the bed, kissed her forehead, and began to check her injuries.

She watched me with a soft smile, "You look adorable when you're worried."

I froze for a moment, then let out a small chuckle. "No one's ever called me adorable before, *Mi Corazón,*" I replied, rolling my eyes playfully. Her smile grew as she reached up to caress my face.

She grazed her fingers along my jaw and that's when I realized how tightly wound I was. I loosened my clenching jaw and blinked at her. She was so beautiful, still. Cuts marring her face did nothing to dim the shine.

Her eyes gleamed with a slight sheen. Her cheek was swollen and I could see bruises forming beneath the soot. The soot.

Fuck.

She had survived a blast. All because she was mine. *Mine.* Leora Mateez was mine and I was falling fast and hard for her.

I gently held her face, being careful of her bruises, and kissed her softly. Her eyes lit up with desire, and she pulled me closer, kissing me back passionately. She wanted more, but I knew she was hurt and needed rest.

"Let's take it easy, *Mi Corazón,*" I whispered, breaking the kiss gently. "We should check your injuries."

Leora exhaled a soft, somewhat playful sigh and complied, stretching out on the bed, a restrained smile tugging at the corners of her mouth. I took my time, gently inspecting and bandaging each wound, ensuring she was as comfortable as possible. After handing her a painkiller, I encouraged her to rest. Her eyes fluttered shut, fatigue overtaking her quickly as I started to tidy up the scattered supplies in the room.

Alone with my thoughts, the dread of nearly losing her gnawed at me. The fear that had clutched at my chest was a visceral reminder of our precarious reality. It was clear now; I had been avoiding the inevitable call to Alpha One. But it couldn't wait any longer. She was determined to be part of this world, and frankly, the thought of her anywhere but by my side was unbearable now.

With the room tidied, I washed my hands and switched off the light, leaving only the dim moonlight spilling through the window to illuminate the space. Stripping off my t-shirt and cargo pants, I slid quietly into bed beside her. Careful not to disturb her, I rested a hand gently on her belly, feeling the rise and fall of her breath—a simple confirmation that she was still here, still with me.

TWENTY-FIVE

Leora

I woke up feeling sore and groggy, the aftermath of yesterday's ordeal still heavy on my body. As I shifted slightly, I felt Zarek's hand resting protectively over my belly. Turning towards him, I found him sleeping peacefully on his stomach, his face turned towards me. I couldn't help but smile as I admired his relaxed features. Almost as if sensing my gaze, Zarek's eyes fluttered open, meeting mine with a sleepy warmth.

"Good morning," I whispered, leaning in to plant soft kisses along his shoulder.

"Morning," he responded, his voice deep and husky.

My kisses wandered up to his neck, eliciting a low groan from him. Reacting swiftly, he propped himself up and caged me gently beneath him, his strong legs and arms framing my body.

"Don't test me, baby. You're hurt, and we're not doing anything until you've healed," he murmured, pressing a tender kiss to my lips before getting out of bed with a grin that left me staring after him in awe.

"You know, you can't look this good and not expect me to want to jump your bones," I called out playfully, propping myself up on my elbows.

He laughed, grabbing a towel and throwing it over his shoulder. "Shower time, baby. Get up."

"Do I smell?" I joked.

"Like soot," he replied, his smile faltering slightly as a shadow crossed his face. He quickly shook it off, scooped me up, and carried me to the bathroom.

After a lengthy shower, we dressed and joined the others for breakfast. Dylan, Kabir, and Amelia greeted us with warm smiles from the dining table, while Logan busied himself in the kitchen with a sizzling omelet.

"Hey, good morning, Leo," Logan chirped, too brightly for my current mood. I was still irked by his earlier behavior, and his cheeriness now seemed forced.

"My name is Leora, remember?" I retorted sharply.

Logan set the pan down and faced me, his expression faltering. "Fuck, I... I'm just..." He struggled to find the right words, a rare sight for Logan.

"I was an ass. I'm so sorry for that. I shouldn't have taken out my anger on you. I was wrong, Leo." He admitted, his gaze dropping to his feet.

Watching his sincere discomfort softened my frustration.

"That wasn't hard, was it?" I said as he quickly

enveloped me in a heartfelt hug.

"I was terrified, Leo. I thought you were fucking dead," he confessed, his voice shaky. "I thought your last memory of me would be me icing you out. Fuck. I thought I'd lose the two people closest to me."

He pulled back slightly, smiling weakly. "Zarek wouldn't be the same without you. So, don't ever fucking die on us, Leo."

I smiled, touched by his words, and kissed his cheek. "Okay, then, no training for me for the next 48 hours," I declared, stepping back to drink my water, a smirk tugging at my lips.

He shook his head, chuckling, and playfully flicked my forehead. "Ow?" I feigned injury, rubbing the spot.

"Shut up, I didn't even flick you that hard," he retorted, rolling his eyes.

I laughed, joining the rest of the squad at the table, and sliding into the seat next to Zarek.

Kabir slid one of the Crazon devices across the table. "They used Crazon to hack our systems and block the alarms and cameras. I traced the connection back to Candor Imports Inc. servers. Jerome Tyson was behind this."

Dylan and Zarek nodded seriously, while Amelia and Kabir looked slightly surprised. Logan walked over to the table and set down six plates, then went back to get the omelets he had made for everyone.

I cleared my throat. "Uh, Kabir? You could've asked me too. I knew Jerome was behind the cameras going down. And Casteel had a new partner named Mason with him. He was short, with a crew cut, ginger, built."

Kabir smiled and turned his tablet towards me.

"Could you have found out that Jerome is now in New York and not in Bali?"

The screen showed a blinking red dot over New York City. I pinched the screen to zoom out and saw a bunch of green dots near Woodstock.

"That's the squad," I whispered. Kabir nodded. "Are you tracking their phones?"

Kabir looked at Zarek, who nodded in approval.

"We all have a chip called RLM-I98, for remote location monitoring," Kabir explained, pointing to his chest near his heart. "It works until our heart stops. A private security firm called Blackthorn created it."

The name *Blackthorn* sounded familiar.

I frowned. "What if someone hacks into it? Wouldn't you all be in danger?"

"Good question," Kabir grinned, turning to the team. "That's why I propose using one of the Crazon devices to secure our systems. It has the capability to hack us, so why not use it to secure us instead?"

Dylan and Logan immediately nodded. Amelia shrugged, indifferent, and Zarek looked thoughtful. After a pause, he spoke.

"I think we shouldn't. We're trying to get rid of these dangerous devices, not use them."

"We need better security, Ghost," Kabir insisted. "I can ask Sebastian from Blackthorn to help. But, right now, Crazon is our best shot. I've already isolated this unit from the server."

"I think we should do it," Dylan supported.

"Yeah, we could ask Alpha One to approve the security protocol," Logan added.

"Alpha One?" I queried.

"Head of Alpha Program, Chief Robert Callahan," Zarek explained. "I agree we need to address these attacks. I'm just not sure Callahan would agree. I'll try to convince him, but don't get your hopes up."

"Should we move again?" Amelia finally spoke up.

After a brief silence, I jumped in. "I think we should stay. Moving is what they'd expect from us, and Crazon is equipped to track us. They might intercept."

Zarek looked at me, his expression a mix of pride and curiosity. Logan grinned. "Look at you, chiming in with expertise. I agree with her."

"We don't move," Zarek decided. "I have a call with Callahan soon. I'll bring all this up."

Kabir added, "We should also chip Leora with the cookie."

"I like the name, 'cookie'," I chuckled.

"Okay," Zarek agreed.

"She'll be sore for a day, Zarek. Can you handle that?" Logan teased, earning a slap on the arm from me.

Zarek winked at Logan and kissed my cheek before starting on his omelet.

✧ ✧ ✧

"There you are," Kabir smiled at his tablet after implanting the chip in me. It was small, about half the size of a grain of rice, but the area stung and was starting to swell.

"Are you okay?" he asked.

"It's fine. This hurts more than getting blown up, though."

Logan snorted from the other end of the table.

"You'll be okay. Look," he showed me his tablet where a new blinking dot had appeared, "Now I can track you if you get kidnapped again."

"I think twice was enough drama for a lifetime," I joked, fanning the sore spot and taking a painkiller with some water.

Zarek was pacing back and forth in the warehouse, talking to Alpha One on his tablet. He stopped and looked at me, continuing the conversation without breaking eye contact, "She's a psychologist, sir, experienced with criminals. She could be an asset to the Alpha Program. Bridgewood will need to approve, but—," he glanced at his tablet and frowned, "Adding to my team is my choice, sir. You never objected to Gill."

Oh lord, he is asking about me joining the squad!

He then walked off to our bedroom and closed the door. I could hear his muffled arguments for ten minutes followed by silence for twenty.

I asked Kabir about Bridgewood and learned it was a discreet name for the United States' new experimental paramilitary operations wing. The Alpha Program was created by Bridgewood and led by Alpha One.

The door finally opened and Zarek emerged with a slight smile, "Mateez 41556, welcome to the Alpha training program. Squad Six is your active-duty location. Carlton 35543 is your training officer."

I just stared at him. I wasn't sure if my jaw survived the fall to the floor. He did it. He finally heard me.

Logan wrapped his arms around my shoulders from behind. Kabir ruffled my hair, smiling, while Dylan nodded at me with his piercing gray eyes.

Zarek looked at me, clearly proud.

"Welcome to the squad, Leora," Amelia hugged

me tightly.

"Training starts at 0700 hours, day after tomorrow, Leo," Logan teased.

Zarek parted the group, wrapped his arms around my waist, and kissed me passionately. When he finally let me catch my breath, he flashed a devilishly handsome smile. "Congratulations, *Mi Corazón.*"

The squad dispersed, laughing and joking, and I realized I was exactly where I belonged. I decided I would get rid of my downtown Toronto apartment tomorrow. Today, I'd just make love to my bunkmate all day and night.

TWENTY-SIX

Zarek

The next day, we all gathered to discuss our next steps.

"I think these shipments are just distractions now. We need to figure out who's handling the exports from China. It can't just be Garret Tyson," Amelia said, looking concerned at her laptop.

"I agree. But since we can't trace the Chinese connections or their motives, we need to keep intercepting shipments to North America. I heard that Squad Two is being honorably dissolved. Brewer and Pedro are the only ones left so..." I glanced briefly at Dylan.

Dylan's close friend, Riley Hayden from Squad Two, along with her teammates Kaylan Bennett and Kyle Deniese, had died in a botched operation in Florida a month ago. This tragedy had reduced their team from five to just two, who weren't combat-ready.

"We should consider getting help from Sebastian's

security firm. They have an intelligence unit that could be useful. I know the CIA worked with them last quarter," Dylan suggested.

"He's a jerk. He wouldn't help us even if it were for saving kids with cancer," Logan muttered.

I frowned at Logan and supported Dylan, "That's a great idea, Dyl."

Logan looked even more annoyed. I didn't fully understand his longstanding grudge against Sebastian Blackthorn.

Kabir had been unusually quiet.

"Kabir? What do you think?" I prompted.

He finally looked up from his laptop. "I'm okay with it. I actually like the guy," he said, staring pointedly at Logan.

"Should Leora and I even bother giving our opinions?" Amelia joked.

Leora cleared her throat. "I've worked with Blackthorn before."

All eyes snapped to her direction.

What? How come she didn't mention it yesterday?

She continued, "God! I don't personally know Sebastian. But I was called to assess an inmate interrogation once. I knew the name, Blackthorn, sounded familiar. The security firm was investigating a case and needed a psychologist to support their interrogation. I worked with someone named Delara Booth. Do you guys know her?"

Lord, she worked with Sebastian's second in command.

The team nodded in unison, their expressions filled with surprise.

Amelia let out a snort, "Leora, Delara Booth is ex-MI6 and basically Sebastian's right hand."

Leora's jaw dropped, and her face flushed a deep

red. "Oh shit!" she exclaimed, her breathing quickening.

"Baby, what's going on?" I asked, noticing her distress.

"I…" she sighed deeply, "I might have called her a bitch right to her face."

Laughter erupted around the table. I joined in, unable to hold back.

"Leo's got balls," Logan commented between laughs.

Leora flicked him on the forehead and then covered her face with her hands in embarrassment.

My laughter was cut short by a faint noise from outside. I turned sharply towards the main door of our warehouse. "There's movement outside. Kabir?" I asked, my voice dropping to a whisper.

Kabir's fingers flew over his keyboard, his brow furrowed in concentration. "There's nothing unusual on the monitors. Wait—" He paused, his eyes darting between the security camera and his screen. "What the hell?"

"Everyone, weapons ready," I commanded quietly as I saw Kabir's alarmed look.

"Our security system just went down," Kabir announced, his voice steady but tense.

I saw Logan pass a Luger to Leora. The rest of us already had our SIG Sauers drawn, aiming at both the front and back doors.

The click of the front door lock echoed through the tense silence. I positioned myself protectively in front of Leora, bracing for what might come through that door.

Leora

I was pointing my gun at the front door as it swung open slowly. My hands weren't shaking, and I was so damn proud of myself.

"Well, that was easy," a low gravelly voice came through the door, followed by a man in a navy three-piece suit. He had chocolate brown skin and his shoulders were wide enough to fit maybe two of me. His face had a hardened look on it that showed he'd probably been through shit. But underneath it all, he was an astonishingly handsome man. He looked like he was Zarek's age, similar build and height.

His relaxed demeanor threw me off, and I gasped as the squad lowered their weapons—I followed suit.

"Fucking hell, Blackthorn," Kabir growled, his eyes narrowing. "What did you do to my security system?"

Blackthorn? Oh God. This was Sebastian Blackthorn, owner of Blackthorn Security, and the man who's second in command was called a bitch by a puny little psychologist dumbass.

Floor, please swallow me whole.

"Sebastian," Zarek nodded and walked over to him, "What kind of speak-of-the-devil entrance is this?"

"Aw, were you talking about me?" Sebastian's smile was twisted with amusement.

The men shook hands, and I caught Logan muttering under his breath, "Zarek, your humor's been dishonorably discharged."

I couldn't help but snort, drawing Sebastian's gaze. He moved towards me, his presence looming like a predator eyeing its prey. Logan instantly stepped in front of me, blocking Sebastian's path.

"Logan Carlton," Sebastian spat the name as though it tasted sour.

"Sebastian. You'll answer to my boss, or you can leave," Logan's voice was menacingly low, a tone I hadn't heard him use before.

"Gunner," Zarek intervened, his eyes darting between the two.

Sebastian gracefully turned on his heel and walked over to the kitchen cabinets like he owned the place. He grabbed a bottle of whiskey like he knew exactly where to find it and poured himself a drink in a glass that he had snagged from another cupboard. A cupboard he knew had our whiskey glasses, of course.

"I fly from New York like I've been summoned by the greatest squad, and this is the welcome I get?" He shook his head and chugged the whole drink.

"It's ten in the morning, Seb. Maybe take it easy," Dylan commented with a wry tone.

Seb? They're on nickname terms?

Ignoring Dylan's advice, Sebastian flashed a grin, then turned to Amelia, winking at her. "Hey, sweetheart! Miss me?"

Amelia's face contorted with displeasure. Kabir, still busy at his laptop probably trying to wrestle back control of our security systems, shot Sebastian a dark look.

Zarek returned to the table, unfazed by the earlier commotion, and resumed eating his breakfast with a casual crunch of bacon.

What the fuck is happening?

"I heard you had run-ins with the Chinese mafia, Gao Ling. His shipments were intercepted and he is *very* angry, boys," Sebastian said, glancing around the room, his eyes finally settling on me with a half-smirk. "And girls."

"So we've got a name now—Gao Ling," Dylan remarked with a nod. "Who is this guy, Seb?"

Sebastian leaned back, considering. "He runs Gao Textiles, keeps his tech developments quite secretive. I hear he's in with President Xi Xiaxu, meets him for drinks weekly. His U.S. contact? Garret Tyson—that's your guy. Gao, though? He's got money that a Saudi Prince would envy, all off the books."

Zarek continued to focus on his bacon, his interest piqued. "And why come to us with this info?"

Sebastian shrugged nonchalantly. "Thought you might need a hand in tracking him down. I've got the tech, you've got the muscle. How about a collaboration?"

"Tell us the real reason, asshole," Logan snapped, his eyes narrowing at Sebastian.

Sebastian, unruffled by Logan's hostility, flashed a grin. "Delara Booth has been on their trail for some time now. It's not just Crazon they're shipping; there are other products going to Japan, India, the UK, and South Korea—all nuclear powers. That can't just be a coincidence."

Zarek's face remained blank. He clearly respected Sebastian, but a slight twitch to his eye told me he didn't trust him fully.

"As the North American division of Alpha Program, we only have the jurisdiction to take down Garret and his son, Jerome. They've been…" Zarek paused, searching for the right word.

"Troublesome? Relentless? Stupid?" I chimed in, attempting to lighten the mood. A ghost of a smile flickered across Zarek's lips.

"Leora Mateez," Sebastian said, turning his attention to me with a lopsided smile.

"So you've heard of me."

"Indeed, the famous damsel in distress," he replied with a teasing tone.

Okay, yeah. I despise this man.

"Am I, though? Maybe your intel is outdated, Mr. Blackthorn, but I recently saved *myself* from Casteel's attack."

His smile widened and he threw his one free hand up, "Yep, it's official. I like this one."

Sebastian closed the distance between us, took my hand in his and kissed my knuckles.

Zarek got up and growled, "Hands off, Blackthorn. She's mine."

Sebastian immediately dropped my hand and raised his brows in a question.

I nodded with confirmation, "Tell us, Mr. Blackthorn. Why haven't you stopped Garret if you knew all this was going down?"

"Asking the right questions is a skill, Ms. Mateez. One you possess," Sebastian sounded amused, "I didn't stop Garret because he may be the one pulling the strings, but the strings are rather hard to track down. We don't know his motive and his son, Jerome, has been handling the shipments. We can take Jerome down tomorrow, but we both know Garret will have a backup ready. Legally, I can't touch him."

"And illegally?" I asked.

He lowered his head to meet my eyes, his face inches away, "Illegally, I can gut him, and strangle him with his own intestines until he is blue and dead."

"That's rather extreme for someone who is just

importing technology products. Or maybe that's not all he does?" I pressed further.

He then turned to the whole squad, "Human trafficking, illegal drug trade in major North American cities, and slavery. Yep, slavery."

The whole squad shifted a bit. Zarek was frowning and Logan's eyes went dark.

Sebastian's nostrils flared and I saw anger, raw anger emanating from him. Perhaps, he was a noble man, after all.

TWENTY-SEVEN

Zarek

"Help us take Garret down and we might be able to collaborate for Gao Ling takedown. I can ask Callahan if we can bypass Interpol," I said. "By the way, why isn't Interpol on this?"

Sebastian shrugged, "They're probably busy with the Russians. But that's a conversation for another year."

"What do you need from the squad?" I asked.

"I need you to operate from New York. I have intel that their next shipments are landing in Florida, New York and Nova Scotia in two weeks. They know you can't target all. New York is the biggest one and it won't just be the tiny little Crazon. If we can locate their holding warehouse, we can find and use Jerome to get to Garret."

"We have confirmation that Jerome is in New York. How many operatives can you spare?" Kabir asked.

"It'll be me, Delara Booth and Zane Cruiser. We're locked in for this assignment. What about you?"

I saw Leora shift nervously.

Nodding at Sebastian I replied, "The whole squad and a trainee. Leora will be a part of this. I can't leave her here and I can't spare personnel for protection."

"I have bodyguards that can look after her, if you want," Sebastian raised a brow.

No. I won't leave her under any protection I didn't fully trust.

Before I could express my opinion Leora jumped in.

"No. I'll be joining you guys," she said firmly.

"Bold woman you snagged there, Rivera," Sebastian smirked.

I gave him a small smile and continued, "Squad Six. Buckle up. We're going to New York in 24 hours."

Sebastian nodded, "I'll get my private jet to collect you all. Kabir? I'll send you the details."

Kabir gave him a curt nod and Sebastian left through the main door as silently as he came.

How did he even arrive here?

I gave the squad one last look and headed to the bedroom. I heard Leora's faint footsteps following me and I smiled to myself.

She was so damn confident today. Her questioning, her steady voice, her defiant eyes, all had my cock throbbing.

✧ ✧ ✧

"God, Sebastian gives me the chills," she mock-shivered as she closed the door behind her.

I caged her against the door, "The way you talked today. The confidence. It's a massive turn on, baby."

Her shiver was definitely real this time.

I whispered against her neck, "I was half hard the whole time. I'm glad others didn't see it."

I caressed her bare thighs, drawing circles over her smooth skin.

"Zarek," she breathed.

"God, why do you wear these tiny little shorts? Showing off these legs to everyone. All I can think is how they'd look wrapped around my face."

"I guess I can manage that," she smirked.

God, this woman.

I knelt down to my knees and in one swift motion, I removed her shorts and panties.

"I need to taste you, *Mi Corazón*," I looked up at her, "I didn't have my breakfast properly."

She giggled and that soft sound went straight to my cock. I put one of her legs on my shoulder and kissed her inner thigh until Leora's hands were in my hair.

"You tease," she whispered.

I smiled against her glistening pussy, taking her in, and then lapped up her juices. She tasted like heaven.

God, I could do this forever.

I could love this pussy, her moans, forever. Fuck, I could love *her* forever.

Sucking and nibbling her clit, I slid a finger inside her and her moans grew into grunts. When her legs started to wobble, I picked up my pace and gently put my teeth on her nub and sucked hard.

She quaked under my arms. One more thorough flick and her release found her. She moaned my name and her legs wobbled so hard that I was afraid she'd fall. I kissed her once more and she shuddered against my smile.

Pulling up her panties and shorts I stood up.

"You're it, Leora. I once told you that I was afraid you might be it," I cupped her cheeks, "You're fucking it."

Her cheeks flushed a beautiful pink and she smiled lazily.

"Zarek Rivera. You're it for me too."

I made love to her then, with all my might. Leora was everything to me. I'd damn the mission if it meant she was mine. I'd damn the consequences if it meant she was safe.

I was in love with Leora Mateez, and I'd damn myself if I let her be hurt again.

✧ ✧ ✧

After an uneventful short flight to New York, we landed on a private strip at the Newark airport. I looked out the window and saw black SUVs meticulously parked right at the tarmac.

Sebastian gave us the cover of being a private security unit from Toronto, out here in New York for business. No one on the plane, staff or the pilot, knew that they had just flown one of the deadliest Alpha squads of the past decade. We were the last ones left. Other squads were either dissolved, non-operational or dead. The missions we had completed, the devils we had killed to save innocent lives, all were a quiet mark on society that we had left. I was incredibly proud of my squad, and now Leora for joining it.

Logan dramatically yawned and stretched as he

descended the stairs of the aircraft. I followed behind him and Leora and others descended shortly after.

"Zarek," Zane Cruiser held his hand to me.

"Zane," I shook his hand, "How have you been?"

"All better after the nasty mission a month ago."

"Heard about that! I'm glad you're doing better, Zane. This is my team, I'm sure you remember."

I gestured to my squad standing beside me.

"Of course!" He nodded and greeted them all.

"And this is my Leora," I tucked Leora in my arms.

"I heard. Delara would be disappointed now that you're taken, Zarek," he eyed Leora and smiled, "Lovely to meet you, Leora."

I smiled when I saw Leora was scowling and I couldn't resist dropping a kiss on her lips.

"Yeah, she *is* a bitch," Leora whispered as we followed Zane, and my smile quickly turned into a laugh.

We headed towards the non-descript cars and Zane asked the staff to load our duffle bags in.

Soon, we were on our drive to Brooklyn. When the Blackthorn Security building fielded into view, I heard Leora gasp. Hell, even I was in awe of the modern brick warehouse that spanned a full two blocks. The three-story structures in each block connected through multiple bridges over the street below.

"Don't let the floors fool you. Underground operations are more... high-end cases. We officially have three levels below these blocks," Zane said.

"And unofficially?" I asked.

Zane just smiled and shrugged like he didn't know the answer. We all got out of the cars in the first-level basement parking and Zane asked us all to follow him through a massive elevator that very well could carry a vehicle inside. The elevator required a thumb print and a code to enter.

Right. A security firm.

The elevator doors opened to a beautiful lobby, with high ceilings, exposed bricks, glass partitions and floor plants adorning every corner. I took in the beautiful space. A massive arch window looked at a covered courtyard right in the middle of the complex.

"We have guest rooms on this floor. Here are the keys you'll need to enter them. The room number is tagged right here on the card," Zane's voice interrupted my shameless exploration, "Settle in, freshen up, and I'll have someone pick you up from right here in an hour."

He nodded at me and stalked off. I saw six keys lying on the reception desk. The woman behind it gave me a nervous smile, tucking a loose hair behind her ear.

I slid one key back towards her, "We won't need the sixth room."

I encircled my hands around Leora's waist and watched the woman's smile falter.

Yeah, Logan was right. I'm oblivious sometimes.

The squad had their keys, and I walked Leora to our room, unlocking the door to reveal a flood of light from the floor-to-ceiling window overlooking the courtyard. The room boasted a massive king-sized bed framed in gold metal, set against dark teal walls—luxury far beyond our usual safehouse digs.

"Nice job, Blackthorn," I muttered under my breath.

Leora, unable to hide her delight, flopped onto the bed with a contented sigh. She seemed to adore this place more than I anticipated.

After freshening up, we regrouped with the squad at the reception, where Delara Booth's voice floated through the archway opposite us. Delara, a petite blonde known for her ability to disappear into a crowd, was someone I'd worked with on several CIA missions. Today, she was all business, clad in a formal blue dress and beige heels that barely made her taller than Leora.

"—let's hold off on sending in the team. I'm still tracking their movements," she was saying into her phone.

As she ended the call and noticed us, her face lit up. "Zarek darling," she greeted, pulling me into a hug with her posh British accent.

"Delara," I responded, feeling Leora's tense presence beside me.

Leora cleared her throat conspicuously, and I quickly stepped back from Delara.

My little possessive Leora.

Suppressing a smile at her barely concealed jealousy, I watched as Delara turned her attention to Leora. "And you must be Leora, Zarek's new trainee," she said cheerfully.

"And his girlfriend," Leora corrected her sharply.

Girlfriend. I like the sound of that.

"Lovely to see you again, Delara," Leora let out her hand. Confusion filled Delara's face followed by a quick recognition.

"You are Dr. Leora Mateez, from the Toronto Penitentiary. I knew I recognized that name," she smiled.

"We call them Detention Centres. And yes, that's me. We worked together briefly a few months back."

"Oh I remember," Delara's smile morphed into a rather mischievous one, "No one has ever called me a bitch to my face before. I liked you immediately."

Leora's eyes widened and she looked at me. I shrugged.

"C'mon, let's get you all downstairs. Zane and Sebastian are very excited to show you what we've got."

She led us to a different elevator, one hidden from general view, requiring both a retina scan and a code. The doors slid open, revealing a descent into the heart of Blackthorn's operations.

As we entered, I saw that this elevator had levels going down to '-5'. It immediately made me wonder if -5 wasn't still the last underground level they had. Perhaps, there was another elevator here with higher security access.

As we descended to level '-4,' the elevator doors parted to reveal a stark transformation from the upper floors. The ambiance shifted dramatically, evoking the interior of a high-tech spaceship. The walls were painted in shades of dark grey and black, accented with sleek silver touches that caught the light as we moved.

"Let's head to the command center," Delara instructed, her voice echoing slightly in the expansive space.

She led us across a sprawling lobby, its sleek black suede couches scattered strategically, offering a stark contrast to the stark, utilitarian design. We approached a corridor ending in a large opaque glass door that looked more like a portal to another dimension than a simple entryway.

After another retina scan and a quick input of

codes, the door slid open with a soft hiss, reminiscent of airlocks in sci-fi movies. The immediate buzz of activity hit us—the rapid clatter of keyboards and low murmurs of concentrated conversation created a background hum of efficiency and urgency.

I glanced at Leora, who surveyed the scene with a cool, impassive gaze, seemingly unphased by the high-tech surroundings.

"This is where the magic happens," Delara said with a hint of pride, gesturing broadly to the sprawling room filled with glowing screens and busy personnel. "Welcome to the nerve center of Blackthorn."

Someone from my squad whistled at the back.

"We need a bigger budget, Ghost. *This* is what I call Command Center. *Damn!*" I heard Kabir.

Delara looked over her shoulder and gave him a wink.

Stepping inside, we navigated past a series of diligently working figures before pausing before a pair of imposing double doors. Unlike the technologically fortified entries we had encountered earlier, these doors were starkly unguarded.

Pushing the doors open, we entered what was unmistakably a conference room. The simplicity of its setup contrasted sharply with the high-tech ambiance of the outer corridors. Sebastian and Zane were already there, seated at the far end of a long, sleek table that seemed to stretch endlessly towards them.

"How was the flight?" Sebastian's voice broke the initial silence, his tone casual yet carrying an underlying measure of formality.

"Comfortable," I responded, my eyes scanning the room.

"Fancy," Kabir added with a chuckle, earning himself a quick, sharp glance from me.

Sebastian smiled at the response, then clapped his hands together, a crisp sound that seemed to command attention. "Glad to hear that, Kabir. Right, let's get to the point. Have a seat, folks."

As we all settled into our chairs, I noticed tablets embedded directly into the table in front of each seat. As if on cue, they powered on, the Blackthorn logo briefly illuminating the screens before switching to a 'Connecting…' message.

"Could you briefly share the agenda?" I asked, directing my gaze towards Sebastian, who gave a slight nod to Zane in response.

"Of course," Zane began, his voice steady and clear. "The agenda of this meeting is threefold: first, to review what we know about Garret Tyson; second, to shed some light on new information gathered by my team; and third, to outline the mission objectives."

"Welcome to Operation Icarus, Alpha Squad 6," Sebastian announced, his voice imbuing the name with a weight that seemed to fill the room.

We all nodded in unison. I returned Sebastian's gaze with a curt nod as the screen in front of me flashed with the words 'Operation Icarus'. The one who flew too close to the sun.

"*We're* the sun in this metaphor, I presume?" Leora asked with a smirk.

"That's right," Delara said with a steely grin.

Sebastian tapped on his tablet and continued, "All right, let's dive in."

Sebastian briefly shared what we already knew about Garret Tyson, his son Jerome, the shipments, and his connection with Gao Ling.

"The new information," Zane took over, "is that the New York shipment will include four new products apart from Crazon. Blast-resistant body armor, thermal-regulating survival suit, anti-radiation medication kits, and customized armored vehicles."

As Zane rolled out the specs and schematics on that ominous-looking screen, the mood turned heavy. I caught glimpses of unease dancing across everyone's faces. Those sketches, too crude for comfort, sketched out more than just vehicles—they hinted at an arsenal on wheels.

Zane's voice cut sharply through the murmurs, "We have intel that the manufacturers were instructed to equip these vehicles with built-in armories, specifically for RPGs."

A murmur of curses swept through the room like a gust of wind shaking loose leaves from a tree. I glanced at Leora, saw her leaning forward, eyes narrowed in focus.

I started to lean in, whispering, "It's an—"

"I know what an RPG is," she cut in swiftly, her voice a hushed whisper, her smile quick and conspiratorial. It made me smile too, reminded me why I leaned on her so much in these briefings.

Then, Delara, ever the show-stealer, swiped the tablet from Zane and took command. "They're gearing up for something big. These aren't just toys for the rich and paranoid; they're fortresses on wheels being handed over to the elite."

Kabir, never one to miss a detail, piped up from across the table, his voice threading through the tense air, "What's odd is the volume of Crazon—just eight to Nova Scotia. It flagged my alerts. Delara, does Blackthorn have a Crazon here?"

The question hung in the air, heavy like a pre-storm silence. All eyes flicked to Sebastian, whose poker face was legendary. Finally, he spoke, "No, we don't have a Crazon here."

He paused, letting the silence swell before he reached into his jacket and pulled out something that immediately drew all our attention. It was a dark blue device, bulkier than a Crazon, with a tiny screen.

"This," he said, holding it up just enough for everyone to catch a glimpse, "is what you really need to see."

Whatever that thing was, it looked like it packed more than just electronic punch.

"You fuckers, you replicated Crazon?" Logan's loud voice cut through. Hell, even I was confused now.

"Logan, listen," Zane pacified, "This device is called Sentrix v5.4. We created it four years ago and upgraded it over the years. This thing is older than Crazon."

"So, you've created another dangerous device?" I asked.

"It's better than Crazon, my friend. Because it has protocols in place to never go rogue. It's built with an algorithm called ADAM. It's basically us showing Sentrix what the bounds of positive humanity are and how to never go beyond it."

I was glad for Zane to dumb it down for the non-tech people in the room. But, even though they tried hard to defend themselves, their explanation only got suspicious looks from my squad.

Sebastian raised his hand, "This is not about Sentrix."

Some of my squad scoffed.

"This is about how we are still in the dark about Crazon's capabilities, we don't know their target countries or locations for the eventual attack, and we don't know the motive or who is pulling the strings," I finished the thought and a faint smile took over Sebastian's face as he nodded.

"Mission objective," Zane boomed, "Is to locate and extract Jerome Tyson, code name Icarus, and question him to get the link to Garret. Along with that, we will be destroying their holding location. We cannot let the wrong people get their hands on these products. Even if Icarus extraction fails, we will be destroying their facility. Now the only question is, where is it?"

TWENTY-EIGHT

Zarek

I walked into our room and saw Leora crouched on the bed, rocking her body looking at the tablet Kabir gave her. She scratched her head and tapped on the screen.

"Yes!" She pumped her fist in the air.

"What are you up to?"

She jolted and her head whipped up.

"God! Make some sounds at least."

"I did," I laughed and sat beside her, "Now, what are you up to?"

I kissed her exposed shoulder. She was wearing a black tank top with gray shorts.

"Studying for the written test. Who knew I'd be a student again at almost thirty?"

I swiped the tablet from her grasp and couldn't help but admire the screen flashing her near-perfect score. Leora, with her razor-sharp mind, had been tangled up in knots over the online exam scheduled for tomorrow. Earlier, I'd taken it upon myself to ease some of that tension, worshiping her with my lips, drawing deep, shuddering breaths as I savored her pussy. Later, I'd left her wrapped in the sheets, her textbooks spread around her like a fortress as she buried herself in study.

"Look at you! Your score is near perfect, *Mi Corazón,*" I kissed her cheek. She took the tablet back and studied the screen.

"I need it to be perfect, not near perfect. Plus there's a whole list of military slang I still need to learn," she frowned animatedly and chanted in a low voice, "Copy. Got your six. Tango Mike…"

I laughed as she continued with a bunch of weird gibberish that even I hadn't heard.

"You googled it, didn't you?" I grabbed her waist and rose above her. Then I pinned her down and caged her with my hands. The tablet fell out of her hands and she cupped my face with them.

"Why are you so fucking beautiful?" She pouted, "Look at those damn dark brown eyes. Ugh. And these lips, even I don't have such luscious lips. And those lashes. You're putting all women who do eyelash extensions to shame. It's like you—"

I stopped her rant, putting my lips on hers.

She thought I was beautiful?

I briefly thought about taking her to the bathroom to show her how beautiful she looked in the mirror. I broke our lips apart and gave her a breathless smile.

"You're beautiful, through and through, Leora. Your smile, your eyes, your mind, your strength, your confidence. Everything is beyond what I deserve."

She flashed me a triumphant grin, her happiness infectious. I leaned in, capturing her lips again, my tongue eagerly seeking hers. A groan slipped from me as she shifted, sinking deeper into the pillows and giving me easier access. I teased her lips gently, drawing a playful tug from her in response.

Suddenly, a torrent of unwelcome images flooded my mind, slicing through the haze of desire. The intensity was too sharp, too familiar to brush aside. My brow furrowed as I battled the intrusion, mentally shoving the memories away, but they clung stubbornly.

Leora's hands stilled, her breath catching as our lips parted. The confusion in her eyes as they met mine told me she'd seen the shadow cross my face.

"What's wrong?" She asked.

I closed my eyes and shook my head, "It's nothing."

"Tell me, Zarek. You look like you've swallowed gasoline."

I reluctantly smirked to lighten the mood, "How would you know what that looks like?"

Her gaze didn't waver.

"Tell me," she urged gently.

My focus was a blur; I shook my head slightly, attempting to clear the fog of memory. "Years ago," I began, the words tumbling out with a tremor, "we were a squad of six."

Leora's hand found mine, her touch a silent encouragement to continue.

"Maxton 'Psyche' Prescott," I said, the name bringing a lump to my throat. "He was an exceptional interrogator, though his combat skills… they could have used some work." I paused, the past suddenly too present. "He didn't make it back from a mission in Egypt. An American archaeology team had been attacked, and we were sent for a covert rescue. But politics were tense, and we walked into an ambush. Kabir barely made it out, and we... we lost Max."

I drew in a shaky breath, feeling the old weight of guilt and grief pressing down on me. "Just now, it all came rushing back. I saw flashes—visions of this mission going wrong. Dylan bleeding out, Logan's body burnt, Amelia in pain, Kabir shot right before my eyes." My voice broke as I confessed, "It's the same nightmare that haunted me after Max's death. And when Zavier... when I lost him, it all turned into real fear."

Unable to bear the weight of her gaze, I moved away and buried my head in my hands, overwhelmed.

"Zarek, look at me," Leora's voice was firm, her hands steady on my back, tracing comforting lines along my spine.

But I couldn't. I just couldn't lift my head, not yet, not while the ghost of those old fears clung to me so tightly.

"Please, look at me," she urged and I couldn't deny that pained voice. I looked at her expecting sympathy or maybe even blame. But her eyes shined with a strange resolve. She managed a small smile and said the words I needed to hear.

"Fear only shows us what we care about, Zarek. You care about them, it's very evident. But know that you're also cared for. I care for you. Your squad cares for you. And we fear for you too. I can't give you empty promises and say nothing will happen. So, feel the fear, Zarek. Feel it, and let it guide you."

Her words found their place deeper in my soul than I thought. Fear was care. Fear was love. And I loved this little family I had. I loved Leora. Fear was having to lose them. Having them lose me. Leora hadn't pacified me. She hadn't rejected my fear. In fact, she asked me to feel it. She made me allow myself to feel it. And in that moment, I knew I had to tell her. Tell her that she was also feared for. Cared for. And loved.

"There was a time, Leora. When I thought I couldn't have anybody fearing for me. And it wasn't too long ago either. That time ended the day a woman dressed in a denim jacket came to my rescue and beat up the bad guys. It was when she willfully showed me she wanted me, unapologetically. It took me a while to realize that I could want her too. Hell, I really wanted to not want her, crave her, love her," I cupped her cheeks, "But it's too late now, *Mi Corazón*."

With trembling lips, she let out a ragged breath, her eyes blinking back tears.

She finally whispered, "I'm falling in love with you too."

I smiled widely at her, "Sweetheart, I'm so far down from falling in love with you, I'll need you to catch up to me."

Laughing softly even as her tears wet her cheeks, she pressed her lips to mine. I deepened the kiss instinctively, my hands cradling her neck. She was my everything, my all. I had fought so hard to keep this distance, to stay away, but in this moment, all that resistance seemed pointless. I knew, now, that I'd rather drown in her, be consumed by her presence, than wander in a world without her light. As I kissed her, the lingering fear dissolved. Each stroke of my tongue, a commitment. Each nibble, a prayer. Each breath, a vow.

Leora

By the time the sun set, I had finished two more mock tests. My score kept decreasing by a few points every time and I was mildly pissed. The landline in the room rang.

"Mateez," I said.

"Hello, Leora," a woman's voice echoed, "This is Greta from the reception. I was told to inform you that your team has assembled in the lounge for a cocktail dinner. We're sending you a dress and your presence is requested in thirty minutes."

"Okay. Thank you, Greta."

Just as I hung up, there was a knock at the door. I climbed out of the bed and opened it. A woman in her forties slid in with a black garment bag, a box that I assumed had shoes, and a makeup bag.

"Thank you," I murmured.

She left and I opened the bag to see a beautiful plain black dress. It had a halter neck and flared below the knee.

There were also black strappy sandals with a low two-inch heel. Having barely worn heels in my whole life, I eyed them suspiciously.

I sighed and headed to the shower. After cleaning myself up, I slipped into the dress and heels, and walked over to the full length mirror.

Damn, you clean up good, Leora Mateez.

I had always worn clothes that were more boyish. Most of my wardrobe back in Toronto consisted of cargo pants, sweatpants, hoodies, and denim. I was pretty sure I had a dress or two cooped up somewhere in there, but I hardly wore them.

I couldn't help but smile at my reflection. I was definitely liking the look, and driving Zarek a bit insane wouldn't hurt, either.

I put on some light makeup and headed to the lounge. I was told it was on the second floor, right above the rooms. As I walked into the lounge, I took in the beautiful decor. Much like the rooms, the lounge had dark teal walls with gold accents. The clusters of suede black couches cut through the color, and I immediately spotted a large black marble dining table with golden legs surrounded by twelve golden chairs. The room emanated effortless wealth. Maybe Alpha one needs to contact Blackthorn's interior designer.

I saw Kabir and Amelia talking to each other and laughing in one corner, with flutes in their hands. Amelia wore a beautiful strapless red dress, showing off her toned arms and her huge falcon neck tattoo. Sitting on one of the large couches were Dylan, Sebastian and Delara. Zarek was chatting with Zane and Logan sat at the bar looking bored. All the men wore dark coloured suits and looked good in them. Hell, they looked irresistible in them.

Zarek had his back towards me when Zane's eyes turned and locked with mine. He smiled and signaled Zarek to turn.

It was almost as though all the air left his body. He didn't move, didn't breathe for a good few seconds and finally took a deep breath. His eyes wandered over my dress that hugged all my curves in the best way, and a sultry smile took over his lips. He strode towards me, his steps determined. I closed the distance too, meeting him halfway.

His arms snaked my waist and his lips brushed my ears.

"You're a temptress, *Mi Corazón,*" Zarek whispered, "Trying to drive me wild?"

"Oh, I'm sorry. Did I do something wrong, Mr. Rivera?" My voice was husky with pure desire.

"Fuck, don't call me that right now," he leaned back to face me. His eyes tracing each part of my face.

"Did I make a mistake again?" I smirked.

"Yes, and you will be punished, Dr. Mateez."

"Oh, is that so? How will you be punishing me?"

"Well, I have a few ideas—"

A throat clearing caught our attention. We both turned and saw Logan wiggling his brows. I was pretty sure both Zarek and I rolled our eyes.

"Leo, you look stunning," Logan walked up to me and almost snatched me away from Zarek and kissed my cheek. I heard Zarek growl.

Zarek snatched me back and tucked me against his chest.

"*Mine*," He scowled.

"Territorial ass," Logan whined.

I stepped out of both their vicinity, "Let me go meet the others...cavemen."

I blew Zarek a playful kiss before drifting over to join Dylan, Sebastian, and Delara. As I settled in beside them, they chimed in with warm welcomes, complimenting my outfit. Dylan stayed silent, but his slight nod spoke volumes. I was beginning to appreciate his quiet nature more and more.

"So, Sebastian," I ventured with a curious tilt of my head, "I heard Dylan calls you Seb. You guys go way back?"

Sebastian chuckled softly, the sound rich and

warm. Dylan cracked a rare smile, and I felt like I'd won some secret prize.

"Yeah, we go way back," Sebastian confirmed. "Dylan was my next-door neighbor after I moved when I was fifteen. We ended up at the same high school and later shared a lot of miserable days in military training."

Dylan picked up the thread, "And yeah, Seb here was always either saving my ass or getting us into trouble. Good times."

Sebastian threw a glance toward Logan, who was deep in conversation across the room. "Logan was my partner for a few training scenarios back in the day. Always pushing the limits, that one."

I leaned in, intrigued by the camaraderie. "So, you guys all served together? With Logan and Zarek too?"

"Not exactly," Sebastian clarified, swirling the drink in his hand. "I ended up in PAG, the Political Action Group, mostly dealing with intelligence and diplomatic cover. These brutes," he gestured at Dylan and then broadly around the room, "stuck with the Special Ops Group. More direct action."

"Interesting," I mused, tapping my fingers on the table. "Then what's your beef with Logan?"

Sebastian eyed me with a slight squint and got up, "That…is a story for another time. And also, not my story to tell. Another round people?"

He looked around the group and their empty flutes. When we all nodded, he stalked off to find another champagne bottle.

"Thanks, Zane. I owe you," I heard Zarek as he walked towards us smiling.

"I'm going to steal my woman for a bit, folks," he said and held his hand out to me. I put my flute on the table next to me and slid my hand in his.

He walked us towards the lounge exit and then took us to an elevator.

"Where are we going?" I whispered, as though we were doing something questionable.

He gave me his most handsome smile, "Shopping."

He swiped a watch near the biometrics screen and the elevators opened up. My eyes widened, "Didn't this have like an ultra pro super uber security?"

He laughed, "I have my ways. Or rather Zane does. This is his watch."

My jaw dropped as he pressed '-4'.

I was trailing close behind Zarek as we veered off the path to the command center, taking a left where I expected a right. A bulky man blocked a nondescript door, eyeing us with clear suspicion.

As Zarek stepped forward to pass, the guard extended a firm hand, stopping him in his tracks. Zarek's glare was met with an equally stern look from the guard.

"Your business?" the man's voice was gruff, a stark contrast to his youthful face. Despite his shorter stature, his broad shoulders gave him a formidable presence.

They sized each other up in silence, the tension thick—then, unexpectedly, both their faces broke into wide grins.

What the hell?

The guard yanked Zarek into a rough, brotherly hug, slapping his back with a booming laugh. "Zarek Rivera! Heard you were back in town."

Zarek clapped him on the shoulder, the irritation melted away by genuine warmth. "Ronan, too long, man," he responded, his voice filled with a mix of joy and relief.

They separated, and Ronan's curious eyes landed on me. "And this must be the famous Dr. Leora Mateez. Never thought I'd see the day Zarek take the fall."

I offered a polite smile, correcting him gently, "Just Leora, please. Nice to meet you… Ronan?"

"Ronan Hayden," he extended his hand, which I shook. "Was in the CIA with Zarek, though we ran in different circles."

I nodded, taking in the connection. Zarek's expression suddenly shifted to something more somber. "Ronan, about your sister, Riley—I should've reached out sooner…"

Ronan's easy demeanor tightened for a moment, a shadow passing over his features. I realized what a small world this was. Riley Hayden was part of Alpha squad 2 and passed away during a mission almost two months ago.

"It's okay, man. You know? It's still very fresh. Dad has been a mess. I told Riley not to join the bloody Bridgewood experimental teams," Ronan paused, "How's uh…Dylan?"

"He's okay," Zarek flattened his lips and nodded.

"Anyway," Ronan shook his head, "What can I help with?"

"Here for some shopping," Zarek gave him a small smile.

"Shop away, my friend," Ronan stepped aside and opened the door for us.

As soon as I entered I gasped. All the walls were lined with backlit shelves, containing guns, rifles and tactical gear that I didn't even have the names for.

"Zane will take care of your licensing. Let's shop, baby."

His hand found the small of my back and he guided me through the massive armory.

"What are we here to shop for? I guess I'm not taking an assault rifle back to the room."

Zarek laughed, "A handgun. We'll get you a nice handgun."

"What do you have?"

"SIG Sauer M17."

"Then that's what I'll get," I smiled up at him.

"There's an M18 as well. It's smaller in size, but basically has all the same specifications. It'll fit these pretty hands of yours," he entwined his hand with mine and kissed me softly.

"Never thought I'd be kissing someone surrounded by guns."

We shared a laugh, our kisses deepening, as he led me through the rifles section, enthusiastically sharing details—many of which I was already familiar with from my training sessions with Logan. Spotting the rifle model I had been using, a surge of excitement rushed through me and I couldn't help but let out a delighted squeal.

Together, we picked up an M18 along with a belt holster and three extra magazines, just to be on the safe side. After dropping our gear off in our room, we made our way back, ready to rejoin the lively atmosphere of the dinner party.

TWENTY-NINE

Leora

"It's simple really," Sebastian passed the potatoes to Delara and continued, "A massive shipment like the one scheduled for New York will have the highest security. It will also have their most capable personnel. I bet Jerome would be at the holding location."

"What are you betting?" Dylan smirked.

"A million dollars," Kabir chimed in.

"Pff...that's nothing," Sebastian huffed.

A round of laughs followed.

"Okay, Mr. Billionnaire," Delara swooped in, "What are our plans to find the said holding location?"

"Ask Zane," Sebastian sipped his wine.

Zane cleared his throat, "That's a bit tricky. I'm targeting all recently rented warehouses near New

York in the past year. I have a list of companies that have rented them and running checks on those. So far, nothing."

"What's plan B? We only have less than two weeks now," Zarek asked.

"Plan B," Zane said chewing on his salmon, "Is to infiltrate their comms. Kabir and I are making tweaks to Sentrix as we speak. We should be able to override Crazon's firewalls soon."

I dove in, "So, once we have the holding location and the schematics, what are our next steps before the mission?"

"*You* will be training, Leo."

I rolled my eyes at Logan.

"Zarek and I have a plan," Sebastian said, "Once we have the schematics, it can be altered. But essentially we'll split into three teams. We need to secure the location and basically replace their team with ours. We'll need one secure entry-exit point that we'll use to extract Jerome. So, team 1 will secure the location internally and plant the explosives, team 2 will be responsible to guard the entry-exit point and act as backup, team 3 will be on extraction."

The whole table nodded. It made sense for us to split the team. I wondered who will be on which team. Before I could ask, Amelia beat me to it.

"What's the split?"

Zarek chimed in, "Sebastian, Delara, Kabir and I will be on one team 1. Logan and Dylan on team 3 for extraction. Amelia and her drones along with Leora on team 2. Zane will be on remote rescue in case all goes to hell."

"I'll bring in the bird as a fail safe," Zane nodded.

"I heard you have VR locomotion technology

here," Kabir eyed Sebastian, "Can we play with it?"

Sebastian laughed but it was Zane who responded, "Once we have the holding location schematics, I plan for us to practice mock missions on it. We have twelve pods, should be enough."

"You and your fancy equipment, Seb," Dylan chuckled, "What *don't* you have?"

"A woman," Delara mumbled and everyone except Sebastian laughed.

After the laughter died down, the team remained silent. There was no sound save for faint clinks of the cutlery.

"I have some good news," Delara broke the silence, "My contact at Vortex Labs came through. We're getting their newly tested and approved military gear. The bulletproof lightweight bodysuit and their new tactical vest. I've ordered twenty of each. They're coming tomorrow."

"Excellent work, Booth," Sebastian smiled, "You're all also getting a wardrobe change, Squad Six. We have a habit of going in with style. So, expect your new gear in your rooms within 48 hours."

Kabir and Dylan were smiling at each other, while Logan wore his persistent scowl as he always did in Sebastian's presence. Amelia nodded at her plate as she chewed and Zarek remained impassive.

We all ate and talked more, and soon our conversations shifted from the heavier topic of Operation Icarus, to lighter topics of American football and ice hockey. The boys laughed and Amelia and Delara chatted. I took a few pointers but overall I remained quiet. Every now and then, I'd feel Zarek's hand on my thigh or a squeeze on my shoulder.

I didn't feel as much out of place, as I felt a bit

intimidated. These were highly trained individuals. They were morphed into deadly weapons for their country, while I was sitting here, at the same table, training to be at least half as good as them.

✧ ✧ ✧

The next day, I stepped out of the small conference room near our rooms. I had just finished my online written test and my nerves were still on fire. I had been extremely anxious, but as soon as I saw the test countdown, I used those five minutes to calm my nerves. I felt a bit relieved, similar to how I felt after a test during my university days. I was pretty confident that I had done my very best in the written test.

The morning sun filtered through the curtains as I entered our room, its early light casting long shadows across the floor. Zarek had been up with me earlier, offering quiet support before we parted ways for my test. Now, the room was empty, the quiet punctuated only by the faint sounds of the facility waking up.

Eager to shake off the last of my test nerves, I decided it was the perfect time to try out my new M18. I strapped on the belt holster and secured the gun, its weight familiar and reassuring against my side. With a determined stride, I headed to Blackthorn's gun range to get in some practice before my official training session with Logan later in the day.

I needed to be completely in sync with this gun. I needed to feel its rhythm, its vibrations, its recoil. I needed to know everything about it.

After turning the safety off, I practiced for three sprints using their practice magazines. With a satisfied grin on my face, I joined Logan near the range in the target practice room.

He whistled as he eyed my gun, "I heard you did some shopping with Zarek yesterday."

"I did," I smiled, "You like?"

"Yeah, it's beautiful. You know you can customize it. Spray it pink or something."

"Black is more my color, Lo," I rolled my eyes.

"Oh, honey, make it yours. Bedazzle it."

"You're weird today," I chuckled and flicked him lightly on his forehead.

"You'll pay for that," he raised his brows.

"Tell you what. If I maintain my high score of 19 over 20, or exceed it, you'll train me in the VR locomotive machine."

"And if you don't win?" Logan asked.

"Then I'll let you flick me on my forehead. Use all your strength."

"I think Zarek will murder me if he sees you need stitches on your forehead," he grinned.

"Fine, you choose."

Logan rubbed his jaw, "If you get anything lower than 19, you can't join Operation Icarus."

"What?" I almost snarled.

He shrugged.

"You don't have the authority to do that, Lo."

"Zarek owes me," Logan's face turned serious, "And I don't want you near a firefight."

"Lo, I am backup. You most likely won't even need me."

Logan looked away from me then and sighed, "I just…it's dangerous, Leo. You're not fully trained. We haven't even practiced full combat, with gear and everything. It's heavy and sweaty," he gave an exaggerated shiver, "And itchy."

"I can handle heavy, sweaty and itchy."

"Fine, then today's training is you, in gear, doing a one-on-one drill. Shoot to kill, and resort to combat if you lose your gun. Blackthorn has a maze room. If you win, you join the mission. If not, then we're not taking you."

I hesitated, but I wasn't going to back down. I wanted to be on the mission.

"Deal. Who am I practicing against?"

Logan gave a sly smirk, "Delara Booth."

"Fuck."

"Indeed," I heard Delara as she entered the room.

"You planned this, didn't you?" I gave Logan a lazy smile.

"Maybe."

Logan left me and Delara in the target practice room. Delara wore a black t-shirt and gray sweatpants. Even though her outfit was casual, she still radiated elegance.

"I'll go change," she smiled smugly at me, "You should too, Doc. Your gear is in changing room 3."

Ugh. What a bitch!

I strode off muttering a string of curses. Why did it have to be her?

I entered the changing room and saw a pile of black clothing resting on the bench, along with a tactical helmet, goggles, boots and gloves.

I braided my hair, slipped on the balaclava, and started wearing the rest of the black colored clothing. I noticed there was no vest which made my brows shoot up. I continued with the boots, the goggles and then finished off with the helmet and gloves. One look in the mirror, and I realized I looked pretty badass. If I had the vest, it would certainly enhance the whole look. I smiled beneath my mask and headed to the maze room.

Delara was already geared up in a vest that had five sensors on her chest, two on shoulders and one on her forehead. She was holding a rifle that pretty much looked like a toy but similar in size in M5.

"Are we playing laser tag?" I asked dryly which earned me a smirk from Delara.

"Kind of," she said as she handed me my vest and the forehead sensor that clicked into the helmet pretty easily.

"Here's your rifle, rivaling an M5 in dimensions, recoil and…" she handed me the rifle and my hand dipped not expecting it to be as heavy as a real rifle, "Weight."

She then turned and headed to a door on the far end of the lobby.

"Where are you going?" I asked.

"Come find me, Doc," she said as she disappeared into the second door.

I exhaled once and entered the door in front of me. The door led me to a narrow white-walled path that turned left at the end. I took my stance, propped up my rifle and stealthily walked towards the left turn. Peering briefly over the corner and finding it clear, I strode towards the open room. There were walls everywhere, partitioning and blocking my view of what's beyond. I had no schematics, no backup, just me. And all I had to do was find and neutralize my frenemy, Delara Booth.

THIRTY

Zarek

My phone buzzed in my pocket as I stood with Sebastian, Zane, and my squad. Logan, I recalled was with Leora for her training session. I wondered how her written test went. She had practiced more than enough times with the mock tests. I was sure she excelled.

I took my phone out of my pocket and saw Logan was calling.

"Gunner, what's up?"

"Zarek, you need to come to the gun range floor. Delara and Leo are in a cat fight over you. Bring the team."

What the fuck?

I informed everybody that we need to head to the gun range floor without giving too many details and we all walked towards the elevators to head upstairs. We had all been in the command centre conference room, going over Zane's findings since this morning.

Why was Leora in a fucking cat fight with Booth? It didn't make sense. When we reached the floor, Logan poked his head out from a room and waved us in.

When I entered and looked at the screen, I had the sudden urge to strangle Logan with my bare arms. But I quickly restrained myself when I saw how meticulous and nimble Leora was on the screen. There was a red label on top of Leora's head on the screen, and a green one on top of Booth.

Logan was watching them scour the maze room to find and neutralize the other and I was in awe of Leora's graceful walk. She looked like a panther on a hunt.

"Do that again and we'll be one person short on the mission," I smacked Logan's head.

The team laughed from behind me and continued to watch Booth and Leora's deadly dance. They were far from each other, but that was going to change once Booth crossed the second wall ahead of her.

Then I saw Leora jerk to a stop and scoot down. Was she panicking?

Then she did something I wasn't expecting. She traced back her steps, circled around a bunch of walls, and came up behind Booth, about two walls away. I knew she didn't have a visual of Booth, but she was pretty close to a sneak attack. Booth's direction remained the same, her back to Leora, and I smirked.

I glanced at Sebastian to gauge his reaction, but his expression remained unreadable. Then his jaw started working up and down at a steady rhythm.

I turned my attention back to the collage of screens in front of us.

"Is she really about to sneak up on an MI6 agent?" Kabir mumbled.

"Shh!" Logan snapped.

"Fuck off, it's just a video feed," Kabir countered.

"I'm concentrating," Logan whisper-shouted.

"You're special forces and you can't concentrate with a little sound?" Kabir whispered, mocking him.

"Shut up!" Logan grumbled.

"Boys…" I drawled, trying to conclude their childish brawl.

Booth walked a little to her left and it almost looked like she was stomping her feet and then stealthily turned right. *Fuck*. She had been trapping Leora. She wanted her to be behind her.

I saw Leora head towards where Booth had turned left but then she stopped. She backed up slowly and swiveled. Booth turned around and strode one wall up, *towards* Leora. Another screen from a different angle, showed Booth expecting Leora to have headed left. But my smartass Leora, had anticipated the trap and had turned right, almost coming face-to-face with Booth.

Booth finally walked further, being only one wall away. They were both behind two walls that were parallel but slightly displaced. Then they both peered the corner at the same time, guns drawn. They spotted each other and fired. Neither making contact. Leora scooted down and peered again.

Booth got out, circled around to come at Leora's back.

Turn around, Leora.
Turn around.
She didn't move.
Turn around, dammit.

"Relax, Ghost," Dylan muttered.

Wait, did I say it out loud?

Leora finally turned around right as Booth came up behind her and they both fired and missed. Neither of their vests lit up with any hits. Leora circled around the wall and now they were both on either side of a single wall. I didn't know if it was fluke, or a calculated decision, but Leora walked to the edge of the wall that she circled around from, poked her head out and saw Booth's back.

Just as Leora was about to point and shoot, Booth turned and charged at her. They both fell, their guns slipped away, and they wrestled on the floor with Booth on top.

"Now, *that's* a cat fight," Logan whistled.

"Sebastian," I said in a monotone, "Can Ronan join Operation Icarus? Because I'm going to kill Logan tonight."

Logan snickered and then shushed me.

Fucker.

Booth landed a punch to Leora's jaw and I winced. In a practiced jiu jitsu move, Leora trapped Booth's legs, grabbed her neck and launched herself until she was on top.

They both paused for a beat and Leora nodded. They both got up, stepped away from each other like they were on time out, and removed their vests and helmets.

Leora rolled her neck and Booth cracked her knuckles as they approached each other. Without any fight, they carefully lied down in the same position as they were before, and continued their fight.

At one point they were side to side on the floor, Leora propped her legs up, and push-kicked Booth.

Booth slid almost a meter and rolled. I knew those legs were strong, but *woah*.

Leora and Booth got enough time to stand up on their feet and start throwing punches instead. They both launched uppercuts, hooks, body kicks, and face kicks, and both of them skillfully ducked and blocked.

"C'mon, Leo. You got this. You've sparred with *me*. Delara is nothing!" Logan growled.

Zane cleared his throat and I swore I saw a smile on Sebastian's face.

Leora ducked and launched a hard uppercut to Booth's jaw and her head snapped back. I could see Booth got angry, because she launched a series of quick combination punches that Leora almost blocked. Almost.

She got hit thrice, once on her ribs, once on her cheekbone, and a straight landed on her throat.

Fuck.

Booth was good.

Leora stumbled back and hit the wall behind her. She paused for a beat, shook her head, and regained her footing.

Then she squared her shoulders, dipped her chin down and tilted her face on one side, like a fucking psychopath.

Ooh, my woman is pissed.

She leisurely strolled towards Booth and I could see Booth was a bit confused. She fidgeted, unable to anticipate what Leora's next move would be. In the blink of an eye, Leora hurled herself at her, and they both tumbled to the floor, starting to grapple.

Leora maneuvered to position herself behind Booth, but Booth wrapped her arm around Leora's neck and squeezed. Leora slid down, slipped out of her looped arm and finished on top of Booth.

There was more grappling, position switches and I lost track of which one was Leora. Their labels on the screen were overlapping each other and both had similar builds.

Finally, one of them had the other in another choke hold. The one getting choked tried getting out, struggling to breathe.

"Wait, who's the one choking?" I asked.

Logan chuckled, "Your woman."

Booth finally tapped Leora's arm and they released each other. They both got up, and shook hands.

Leora won.

I couldn't grasp the fact that my Leora had just won against a former MI6 agent. She did take a few painful hits, but came out on top. I was so damn proud of her.

I sprinted out of the room and found her stepping out of the maze room. She removed her goggles and balaclava and I got to look at her beautiful face, now red with combat and adrenaline. Her hair was in a braid and she smiled through her heavy breath. Booth followed next and patted her on her shoulder.

"You deserve it, Doc," Booth said before taking off.

Leora spotted me and her smile widened into a full grin as I smiled back at her. She ran to me and jumped into my arms, wrapped her legs around my waist.

"Fuck, baby, you won!" I kissed her hard.

"I noticed she had," she said between kisses, "a weak grapple. She can't handle herself on the floor."

"*God*, you're so fucking amazing."

"Did that turn you on?" She said breathlessly.

Fuck, this woman is a temptress.

"What if I say yes?"

"Then I'll tell you that I need a shower, and I need some help in there."

She smiled at me and her eyes lit up. Her gaze dropped to my lips and I lost it as I always did with her. I pinned her against the wall and caught her lower lip between my teeth.

"Don't make me think of you naked when we're so far away from our room," I whispered.

"Then take me here, in one of the rooms."

"Fuck, Sebastian has cameras everywhere, baby," I pressed my hard length against her.

"Then let's hurry and get to our room," she kissed me deeply but quickly and jumped back on the ground.

We ran back to our room, and before we could lock the damn door, Leora knelt down and started opening my belt buckle.

"Fuck, *Mi Corazón*," I grumbled.

"I want you, Zarek," she panted as she freed my cock, "I want to taste you."

I couldn't help but smile at the sight in front of me. My Leora, in gear, kneeling in front of me, and ready for my cock. *Fuck.*

"I want you to fuck my face, Zarek."

And those were the words that undid me. My face hardened and I tipped her chin up with my hand.

"Bed. Now," I saw a lazy smile on her face. She sat on the bed, slid back and turned around.

"Lie back down and let your head tip back on the edge," I commanded.

She did so and smiled. I lined my cock with her lips and she opened up for me.

"Tap my thigh if it's too much, baby."

She nodded, hunger in her eyes and I edged in the head of my cock in her sweet mouth. I felt her tongue swirling the tip and I almost came from the sensation.

Fuck, this woman makes me lose control.

I pushed my cock further into her mouth and her lips dragged along the length in the most delicious way. I pushed further until my balls almost hit her nose and I saw the bulge in her throat.

"Fuck, baby, you look so beautiful taking my cock."

A gurgling sound came from her and I pulled out slightly. She didn't tap my thigh, so I continued to slowly watch the bulge appear and disappear as I gently thrusted inside her mouth.

She grabbed my thigh from both her hands and made me almost slam my cock in her and I cursed.

"You'll drive me crazy if you do that," I said breathlessly.

She squirmed happily and did it again. And again. And again. *Fuck.*

Stars swarmed my vision, and I spilled into her mouth. A guttural groan vibrated through me and I felt her warm mouth take my spill in.

"Fuck, Leora," I growled.

I pulled out and she swallowed it all with a happy sigh.

"Baby, that was…"

"Amazing," she smiled.

I knelt down in front of her and kissed her sweet mouth.

"Are you wet underneath all that gear, my Leora?" I asked as I smiled down at her.

"Always wet for you, always," her voice husky.

We both got up and I helped her get out of her gear. As soon as her black lace lingerie came into view, my unruly cock hardened again.

Greedy bastard.

THIRTY-ONE

Zarek

My vision was engulfed in red, and as I opened my eyes, the chandelier above the bed cast a pulsating red glow, bathing the entire room. My eyes widened at the silent code red. The lack of sound indicated that the alarm was meant to alert us without notifying the intruders.

Leora was draped against me, still in deep sleep. I slowly put my palm over her mouth and whispered in her ear, "Get up and don't scream, baby."

She moved a bit and my hold tightened on her mouth. Arms flailing, she panicked and then immediately relaxed as her gaze found mine. I looked at the clock on the nightstand. *3:24 AM*.

"Something is happening. Get yourself armed."

She nodded and we both silently climbed out of the bed. Once armed, I slowly turned the knob of our door and as the lock made a click sound, I hissed.

Fuck it.

I swung the door open and peered out. The lobby was clear. As we passed other rooms, I saw their doors open slowly. After a few false alarms and some curses, my squad gathered and trooped through the lobby and towards the elevator. I kept a close eye on Leora as we walked forward in the darkness. Using the watch that Zane had thankfully programmed for me, I opened the elevator, and we descended to the command center.

The '-4' floor was a flurry of noise as opposed to the top floors. It seemed the danger hadn't reached this floor yet. We all concealed our guns and headed towards the command center.

Zane was hammering on his keyboard, Sebastian was standing beside him with his fingers pinching the top of his nose, and Booth was standing next to him cursing at her phone.

"What's our six?" I asked.

Sebastian stepped towards us, "Our comms have been obliterated—"

"Intercepted," Zane corrected him, holding his index finger up.

Sebastian continued, "While trying to infiltrate their comms, we led them right to us. This is a disaster—"

"Eh…barely an obstacle," Zane interjected calmly.

"Are they physically here?" I asked.

"Not yet," Zane responded, "But they've narrowed down our location to anywhere between

Toronto and Boston. I threw them off their kilter a bit," he then looked at Sebastian, "Not Brooklyn. Not Flatbush. Not Blackthorn. They have an estimated range of us being anywhere inside some 10% of US landmass. We're fine!"

"It's a fucking code red," Sebastian bellowed.

"I'm a paranoid person. Even the slightest insurgence will trigger a code red," Zane said.

"How the fuck are you so calm?" Kabir's voice belied his irritation and Zane simply shrugged.

"Then what code tells us that the enemy is breathing down our necks?" Leora asked, her eyes wide.

"Uh, that'd be code black. The building will sound an alarm and all passages will lock down except for floors below '-3'. It's simple really," Zane shrugged and I had the sudden urge to roll my eyes.

"So, we're fine?" Logan asked, rubbing his eyes.

Sebastian gave him a disgusted glance, "Maybe."

"Oh, fuck yes!" Zane jumped in his chair and pumped both his fists up.

"What?" Sebastian asked.

"Don't be mad, bossman," Zane laughed, "But I sort of planned this. I mean, I didn't expect it to trigger a code red and disturb your beauty sleep, but I had left something traceable for their team to find. Think of it like a fishhook. Yes, it could lead them right to us, but if they grab it, we can trace that signal. Or fish, whatever."

"So, you found the holding location?" I sighed.

"Warehouse unit 67, Port of Brooklyn," Zane smiled.

Tension rolled off of me and I breathed a sigh of relief.

"Fucking hell, Specter!" Sebastian mumbled.

Leora looked up at me, "Call sign?"

I nodded. Leora's eyes sparkled with excitement. "What's going to be my call sign?" she bounced on her heels, her voice tinged with anticipation.

I wrapped my arms around her waist, a smile playing on my lips. "I'm not sure yet, *Mi Corazón*. What do you think suits you?"

Before Leora could answer, Booth chimed in with a smirk, "How about 'Doc'?"

I expected Leora to scoff at the suggestion, especially coming from Booth. But to my surprise, a genuine smile spread across her face. "I like 'Doc'," she declared, looping her arms around my neck.

"Well then, Leora 'Doc' Mateez it is," I said, sealing the new title with a kiss.

"Get a fucking room," Logan yawned.

"Seriously," Zane chimed in.

"We were just in there until you dragged us out," Leora snapped and a fit of laughter erupted.

"Since I'm already up, I'll work with you, Zane," Kabir trudged towards the chair next to Zane and plopped down yawning.

"Rest of you, get some sleep," Sebastian said, "We'll meet at 0700 hours with schematics and start the brainstorming."

We all nodded and headed back to our rooms. I saw Amelia stay behind and curiously look at the screens in front of Zane and Kabir.

As we collapsed on the bed in our room again, I heard Leora whisper something to me.

"What was that, baby?"

Then she grumbled angrily, "Argh! I said I love you, Zarek 'Ghost' Rivera."

I laughed and hugged her close, "I love you too, Leora 'Doc' Mateez."

I kissed her temple and we both slowly drifted off to sleep with our arms wrapped around each other.

✧ ✧ ✧

"How about—" Amelia started.

"Wouldn't work, dammit!" Kabir raised his voice and Amelia uncharacteristically flinched.

"Stand down, Kabir," I glared at him.

The team was gathered in the command center conference room. We had spent almost two hours detailing the schematics and assuming Jerome had full-scale security, we hadn't figured out a way to penetrate the warehouse undetected.

The rectangular structure, spanning two blocks, had four large entry gates on each side and eight loading docks on the east wall. We were going to wait 12 hours for all the shipments to be secured in the warehouse.

"There has to be a way to sneak in without alarming the external guards," Sebastian mumbled.

Leora was no longer looking at the schematics projected on the wall. She had her head down and was staring at the tablet in front of her, lazily tapping away.

"I have a feeling that we may need to take the abrupt approach," I started, "How about we land on the roof and enter? Zane can take us on the bird."

"The roof…" Leora muttered under her breath and then aggressively tapped on the tablet.

"That could work. But we would just alarm their team. Who is to say they're not using RPGs to protect their grounds?" Zane responded.

"And I won't have a safe sneaky place to operate my drones from," Amelia added.

Sebastian rounded the corner of the table and said, "We surely can't extract Jerome this way."

Leora finally let the tablet go and sank back into her chair, her arms crossed. She had a small smile on her face and looked awfully pleased.

"Spit it out, Leo," Logan said.

She connected her tablet to the projector and pulled a map of something I couldn't fully understand. She zoomed in on an area that was labeled 'Channel 415' and the blank space above it was labeled 'East River'.

"So this," she declared, "Is the map of underground tunnels that were closed off in 1961. A few entries and exits span throughout the Port, that some warehouses now use for secondary storage. There's a manhole in Warehouse 67. We just need to find a way to enter from it. Sneakily."

"Damn!" Logan whispered.

"Thank fuck," Kabir ran his fingers through his hair.

"Zane," Sebastian commanded.

"Yeah, I'm checking which ones are closest and whether they're obstructed or not," he tapped away, "Got it. There's one entrance approximately a mile from the warehouse. We can trek through and enter Warehouse 67…" he tapped some more, "From the manhole situated near the south wall."

"Good work, Doc," I said and kissed Leora on the cheek.

"So, now we know how to enter the warehouse," Booth started, "Which walls and pillars we need to place the demolition charges on, and how we're splitting the team. Any progress on locating where Jerome could be?"

"He could be," Zane responded, "Wait, let me pull the schematics again," he tapped away, "Here we go. He could be in the offices situated on the west wall, one floor up. Or he could be on patrol. The biggest office according to this map is Room 4. Looks like a conference room. I could be wrong."

I studied the schematics, "It's right next to the stairs. Should make things easier."

"Zane, load this into our VR locomotive. I need at least 5 different guard rotation scenarios," Sebastian demanded, "and plan surprise attacks."

"On it, bossman!"

"And go get a shower, Zane," Sebastian added as he walked out the door.

Leaning towards Leora, I whispered, "I'll be right back, okay?"

I followed Sebastian out the door and when he saw me behind him, he signaled me into his office. I sat across from him, a massive wooden desk between us.

"You think we will succeed?" I asked.

"I think we have a very good chance of getting Jerome…alive."

I leaned forward, resting my elbows on the desk, "I think we should focus on getting the team back…alive."

"You're in love," he nodded speculatively, "Don't let that blur your vision, Ghost."

"I love my squad too, as I'm sure you do too, your team. We have bigger fish to fry and I don't want us to make mistakes."

He leaned back in his chair, his head thrown back, and stared at the ceiling, "I think we're missing something. I'm not saying this is all too easy. But I feel like there's something we're overlooking," he abruptly straightened himself and narrowed his gaze, "Did anything unusual or unexplainable happen since you started this assignment?"

I processed back to the time I was shot behind the second safehouse.

"We had a lone visitor at one of the safehouses," I frowned, "He had a sniper gun and didn't approach the safehouse. Logan said he was a hired gun. Logan, Leora and I had been out at that time. Any one of us could have been the target."

"You think it was Casteel targeting Leora again?"

I shook my head because I didn't really believe it. Casteel's aim was to eliminate the squad using Leora. He wouldn't gain anything from having Leora shot. Plus he liked to do his dirty work himself.

"No. That's not it."

Sebastian nodded slowly and I continued, "Well, we had the mercenary questioned. He mentioned a target. Didn't say who it was. At the time I thought it was Leora. But, now I think it wasn't."

Sebastian sighed, "Anything else happen?"

I shook my head, "We can look into this after the mission. We haven't had any problems since then," I said.

"Okay."

"I'll see you at lunch," I got up.

"You won't. I have a meeting with the NYPD."

"Later, then," I said as I stalked off and joined the rest of the team in the conference room.

THIRTY-TWO

Leora

"Before," I said.

"After," Logan rolled his eyes.

I flicked him hard on his head. He hissed and scrunched his brows.

"I said, after, Leo. You can't have the mock mission before the damn mission. You might be out of action for a while after the mock," Logan said sincerely.

I contemplated what he was saying. We were working together to load our gears with maximum effectiveness in the armory. We had plans to figure out how to arm our forces with the best, yet, lightest weapons and keep the team quick on their feet.

"Fine," I sighed, "I'll just do the mock in a month, then. If I'm doing it after Operation Icarus, I'd rather do it with the most preparation."

He nodded as he smiled victoriously, "Good, I'll

whip up your training schedule for after the mission. Be careful though, it'll be super tough with vigorous training and long hours."

I curtsied, "Bring it on, Master Lo."

A shadow passed through his face and his eyes became unfocused. He shook his head and slid three M5 magazines in my vest, along with two knives and five M18 magazines.

"How are you feeling? Light?" He asked.

I did a boxer's skip and shadow boxed. Then I grabbed the M5 rifle from the table and did ten squats.

I nodded, "Feels okay. I think I can manage with more magz. Or even the 21-round magazine for my baby."

"Now, now. Calling your gun a baby makes you exactly like me," Logan laughed as he replaced my previous M18 magazines with the 21-rounds.

"I don't mind being like you, Lo. You may be inappropriate sometimes," he made a face as I continued, "And maybe even outrageously stubborn. But you're loyal, powerful, and a damn good brother to Zarek and Dylan."

He stepped closer to me and rested his hands on my shoulders. His expression, one of deep agony.

"I'm not...it's not just Zarek and Dylan that I'm a brother to. It's you too, Leo. Remember that."

"You think I'll die on this mission, don't you?" I whispered and dropped my head to my chest.

"You're strong, capable, and hell of a fighter. I don't doubt you'll protect yourself. But things can go wrong, very wrong, and you may not be ready."

I met his gaze, my eyes brimming with unshed tears. As they began to blur my vision, I quickly looked away. But then he pulled me into a hug.

"Just stay away from the firefight. If there's backup needed, then let Amelia handle it. I can't lose you. We can't lose you, okay?"

I could no longer control the sudden urge to sob. Tears flowed down my cheeks and Logan leaned back to wipe them away. Suddenly the door opened and Zarek strode in.

He jerked to a stop, his eyes widening, "You made her cry?"

"I…no…I was just," Logan fumbled and Zarek grabbed my elbow and consumed me in a tight embrace.

"What did you do?" Zarek snarled.

"Nothing. I just said that I can't lose her."

I sniffed and added, "He also said that I'm like a sister to him. That blew the damn flood gates."

I heard Zarek chuckle and hold on to me a little tighter.

"You said I'm next?" Zarek asked.

"Yep," Logan's voice cracked slightly and he cleared his throat, "Leo, you're ready with the best arrangement. I'll work with Zarek next."

I nodded, got out of Zarek's arms, and started taking my gear and uniform off. Once done, I kissed Zarek hard and fast.

"Bye, Lolo," I smiled at Logan and he made an annoyed sound as I left the armory.

✧ ✧ ✧

Days passed by in a blur of training, mock missions on the VR locomotive, and intense planning and reiterations. We had multiple contingencies in place.

Out of the twenty-eight mock missions we did, I was only needed for two for Icarus extraction. Logan was playing point on extraction with Dylan as his backup and cover. I was the backup of the backup. Logan and Zarek were slightly pleased that they might not need me after all, which only made me groan.

T minus twelve hours to Operation Icarus

"There it is," Zane pointed at the projection on the wall showing live satellite feed of the warehouse, "Sixteen trucks rolling in and dropping off the shipment."

"Most of them contain armored vehicles, I presume. Do we have a number?" Sebastian asked.

Zane shook his head, "We can expect at least ten of them to contain the vehicles. Assuming there are two in each, that gives us twenty armored vehicles. But that's just an estimate."

T minus two hours to Operation Icarus

Zarek walked over and whispered something to Sebastian and he nodded.

Zarek rested both his hands on the conference table and then his voice filled the room.

"Alright, team, this is it. The moment we've trained for. Every drill, every mock, it's all been leading to this. Rely on your teammates. We stick together, we fight together, and we win together."

"All right, Captain America," Logan smirked.

Zarek clapped his hands together once, "Squad Six, report for Operation Icarus and gear up."

Every one of the Squad Six members stood up, hands to their side, looking straight ahead.

"Carlton 35543 reporting active, show me go." Logan bellowed, a mirth in his voice.

"Rivera 32577 reporting active, show me go," Zarek went next.

"Desmond 39901 reporting active, show me go," Amelia said.

"Gill 34249 reporting active, show me go," Kabir chimed in.

Dylan went last, "Desmond 39900 reporting active, show me go."

Then, all eyes snapped in my direction. I realized then, what they expected from me.

Fuck. I'm part of this squad, aren't I?

I hesitated for a moment and stood up, "Mateez 41556 reporting active," I looked at Zarek and smiled, "Show me go."

Zarek let out a heavy sigh and smiled back. A sense of pride filled my chest. I was incredibly proud of my squad and being part of such an elite team made my heart pound hard. It could have been nerves, or anxiety, but I decided to identify it as excitement and determination.

"I do *not* miss those days," Sebastian chuckled.

The team split into two, men and women, and we headed to gear up on the ground floor in the Mobilization Bay. I saw three black X6s parked inside the building with dark tinted windows and no license plate.

Situated near the cars, were two rooms opposite each other. Amelia and Delara asked me to follow them to one and the men strode into the other one. The room was filled with our gear already placed meticulously. I slid into the full-body bulletproof suit and then put on the all-black uniform. I geared up, put my vest on and got out before putting my helmet on. Amelia and Delara were already outside, fully dressed, hovering near a large desk that had nine small cases sitting on top along with our weapons and magazines.

The doors to the men's room opened and out walked all six of them—Zarek, Sebastian, Dylan, Logan, Zane, and Kabir. They were all fully geared. Their faces were invisible behind the ridiculously badass black balaclavas, helmets and goggles.

Zarek and Sebastian had omitted the full-sleeves black shirt and replaced it with a plain black t-shirt that was too damn temptingly tight on their biceps.

"Holy mother of God of all that's hot and sexy," I mumbled.

I heard Delara chuckle, "You'll get used to this."

I realized that I probably looked like a penguin with my helmet off, so I quickly put it on and clicked the strap under my jaw, hoping I looked half as badass as them.

Then I continued ogling Zarek and his strong tanned arms, his veiny forearms, and strong thighs.

I get to make love to this man.

I shook my head to stop thinking about a naked Zarek, doing deliciously sexy things to me. *Fuck.*

Get a grip, Leora.

Amelia whistled and laughed beside me.

"Stop eyeing them," I whispered to her, "There's your brother in there somewhere."

She exaggeratedly shivered, "Yeah, I'm avoiding looking at the hulk, don't worry."

Zarek strode towards me and that's when I saw a

small label between his fingers. He placed it on my chest on the left and I saw that it said 'Doc' on it. I scanned the room and saw everyone had a call sign label on their chest.

I smiled behind my mask but I was sure he could see my eyes twinkling as he hugged me and kissed me with two layers of masks between us.

"You look sexy as hell, Doc," he said and I laughed.

"You can barely see me."

He joined me and laughed softly.

"All right, team," Sebastian called out, "Grab your earpieces from this box. Get armed and load up in the X6s. Kabir, Zarek, Delara and I will carry the charge backpacks. Dylan, you get the backup charges."

The team nodded and I picked one of the tiny boxes. As I opened it, I saw it had an even tinier device in it. It was as big as a kidney bean. I put the earpiece in and it pinged immediately, before going hear-through mode.

"This is Ghost, radio check, over." Zarek's voice sounded in the earpiece.

"Ghost, this is Gunner, Lima Charlie, over." *Logan*.

"Gunner, this is Falcon, Lima Charlie, over." *Amelia*.

"Falcon, this is Cipher, Lima Charlie, over." *Kabir*.

"Cipher, this is Specter, Lima Charlie, over." *Zane*.

"Specter, this is Ranger, Lima Charlie, over." *Sebastian*.

"Ranger, this is Titan, Lima Charlie, over." *Dylan*.

"Titan, this is Shadow, Lima Charlie, over." *Delara*.

"Shadow, this is Doc, Lima Charlie, over," I ended the radio check and the team nodded, arming themselves.

After a few seconds of silence and everybody eyeing each other, Sebastian's voice echoed in the Mobilization Bay.

"Roll out, people!"

We poured into the X6s. I stuck with Amelia and Zane while others settled into their cars. The engines roared and when the garage doors opened tall and wide, the cars screeched out and joined the traffic.

A sense of irrefutable dread burned through me. I took deep breaths and closed my eyes to get my shit together. I was not going to let the nerves get the best of me. Not today.

Zane pushed a button on the dash, "This is Specter. Channel 415 entry point ETA is in 34 minutes."

"Copy," Logan's voice came through.

"Copy," Dylan joined.

When we reached the location that was a mile trek away from Warehouse 67, we saw multiple NYPD's cop cars swarming the manhole near an alley.

"Don't mind the blue, I called them," Sebastian's voice came through the car's comms.

All of us, except for Zane, streamed out of the cars and gathered around near the cops. Zane reversed his car and drove off to the nearest private helipad where our rescue bird was waiting.

"Thank you, Officer Lee," Sebastian shook hands with one of the officers on scene, "We could really use your help."

"Too many favors, Blackthorn. You owe me a drink," Lee laughed, "Or maybe ten."

"Looking mighty sharp, Mr. Blackthorn," a female officer joined their conversation. Sebastian went a bit stiff.

"Officer Grayson," he nodded, "Are you the one patrolling the alley?"

"Indeed, I am," she spoke in a low voice. Something about her gaze told me she was either pining over Sebastian, or imagining stabbing a voodoo doll of him. I couldn't quite figure it out.

"Ranger, time," Zarek mumbled.

"Right. We're heading in," then Sebastian turned to Officer Grayson, "Don't fuck up, Grayson."

Grayson gave him an amused smile and we all walked over to the open manhole, our flashlights in our hands. Sebastian climbed in and spoke through the earpiece, "All clear. Proceed."

We all jumped in one by one. I followed in last and felt hands on my hips as I hung from the manhole. Zarek helped me down and kissed through the mask again.

"Shame that I can't feel your lips, *Mi Corazón,*" Zarek whispered and suddenly I wished I could see his face.

"Good luck, Zarek. Come back to me in one piece," we clunked our helmets together, a brief respite from the chaos that was to follow.

"I love you, Leora." He whispered. Unfortunately for him, the whole team heard him through the earpiece. His declaration was followed by a series of 'aw's and 'ew's.

I saw him roll his eyes behind the goggles, "Sentrix mute."

"Too late for that, Mr. Rivera." I chuckled.

I saw his eyes crinkle with laughter and he pressed another masked kiss on me. "I fucking love you, Dr. Leora Mateez. Please, don't let me fall."

I nodded gently, my gaze never leaving his, "I love you, Mr. Zarek Rivera. And I won't."

I didn't bother muting, but no one responded in my ear. Our bubble burst just as Zarek unmuted himself.

"Ghost, lead," Sebastian said and Zarek strode off ahead of the group.

I clipped the flashlight to the side of my helmet and remained at the back of the spear formation, closely stepping forward with Amelia.

The tunnel was now slightly lit and I could see how ill-maintained the tunnels were. The cement was cracked and jagged, the walls were damp and humidity filled the narrow space. We came across a path crossing ours, and Zarek held up a fist. Logan and Dylan peered through and swiftly angled their gun towards the left and right side of the crossing path.

"Gunner, left side clear."

"Titan, right side clear."

We continued on. Every now and then Amelia and I would turn back and study the darkness. No one had followed us in. No one was anticipating our arrival. After the mile trek, we finally reached the manhole underneath Warehouse 67.

THIRTY-THREE

Leora

"Titan, take the ladder out," Zarek's voice was barely audible but the earpiece amplified the sound a fraction.

Dylan slid one strap of his backpack out, reached into it and revealed a ladder that was collapsed into a small cylindrical shape. He opened it up and assembled it within a few seconds.

Sebastian bent down and propped Delara over his shoulders. Delara was now sufficiently close to the ceiling of the tunnel and was silently pushing the manhole cover upwards. The short screeching sound of metal against concrete made me wince. We couldn't afford to be heard.

"Hold on, folks," Delara said in her signature British accent.

She finally propped the cover up enough that light streamed in the darkness of the tunnel. Carefully sliding it off, she poked her head out of the hole and looked around.

"Team, we're clear to head up. We'd be in an aisle of goods spanning east to west. I don't see any mercenaries," she said.

Dylan handed over the ladder to Delara and she temporarily fixed it over the rim of the manhole.

It was go-time.

Sebastian and Zarek were the first to disappear into the light. Then Kabir and Delara followed them. This was team 1. They were supposed to clear the internal space and hide demolition charges throughout the warehouse.

Logan climbed up shortly after, followed by Dylan. Team 2. They were going to head upstairs and extract Jerome Tyson, preferably alive.

Then there was me and Amelia, manning the rally point, aka the manhole. Amelia settled down with her tablet in her hand. She reached for something in one of the pockets of her pants and slapped it on the wall. The small square glowed a faint yellow giving us a visible range of at least ten meters across.

Amelia's drones were ready for takeoff. She had them concealed in her backpack. It took her a few seconds to assemble and then she was ready to support the team. She handed them to me to place the small drones on the ground level through the manhole. The body of the drones was as big as my palm and each had four small propellers.

I climbed the ladder and out of curiosity poked my head out to see what entailed above the darkness. There was a long aisle packed with boxes, going high up to almost twenty feet. The manhole was right in the middle of this aisle. I placed the drones on the ground, and proceeded to put the manhole cover back in place as planned.

"This is Falcon. Hawk and Eagle are now active," Amelia said, "Team 2, confirm assistance."

"Confirming assistance for the second floor," Dylan uttered.

I propped my rifle up, keeping myself on alert and ready. I realized I could be needed at any moment.

"Eagle inbound," Amelia tapped and slid her fingers on the screen, "I've got heat signatures spanning the whole lobby of the second floor. Approximately ten to fifteen, Titan."

"Copy," Dylan responded.

Then I heard the unmistakable sound of gunfire. *Shit*. My chest tightened. We were hoping to stay covert for longer. What if this was Zarek in a firefight?

"This is Ghost. Demolition charges to the south wall, complete. Team 1, report," Zarek's voice came through.

I breathed a sigh of relief. Zarek was fine. *For now.*

"This is Cipher, held up, north wall charges half-way through," Kabir said. His voice had a little strain in it and I saw Amelia stare blankly toward the wall in front of her. It was only for a second and then she focused back on her tablet.

"This is Ranger. West wall complete," Sebastian's rough voice came through.

"This is Shadow. East wall half-way through," *Delara.*

Minutes ticked by. More gunfire sounded.

Suddenly there was a faint thud. It came from the manhole. Was the rally point compromised?

"This is Doc. Is anyone at the rally point?"

'Negative's came through rapidly and I shared a look

with Amelia. She promptly adjusted one of her drones' location.

"There are two mercs right above us."

Shit.

Before I could think of what to do, the cover started sliding.

"Stay back, Falcon," I whispered to Amelia and nodded at the wall light. She turned it off and we were shrouded in darkness.

A rifle barrel poked inside the half open manhole and bullets peppered the ground.

I ignored the drumming of my heart in my throat and shook my head.

Now is not the time to panic, Leora.

I could no longer see Amelia's silhouette but I saw her rifle's barrel prodding out of the edge of the light from the manhole, aiming directly at anyone who dared enter the tunnel.

I swiftly jumped and grabbed the barrel of the rifle poking in and let it drop to the ground. The cover opened fully and another set of bullets came. I dodged the rain of bullets and returned fire, followed by a strangled grunt.

Good, it hit someone.

"Doc, is the rally point compromised?" Zarek asked as I was still returning fire.

"We have two mercs," I fired more without using too much ammo, "Converged. Falcon, are there more coming?"

"Negative," Amelia said.

Phew.

The gunfire ceased for a few seconds and I slowly and silently walked towards the manhole. As soon as I saw a pair of legs, I fired again and the merc fell to the ground. I waited for a beat and climbed up slowly. I pushed the gun barrel out and fired in both directions, hearing groans and gurgling sounds in response.

I finally climbed up fully to see the aftermath. Two men were sprawled near the hole, one of them unconscious. Whipping out the zip ties from my pocket, I tied their hands behind their backs. I dragged them away from the manhole so as to not give the location away.

I stayed on the ground level of the warehouse, leaving Amelia in the tunnel, staring at the now covered up manhole.

Then I climbed up five rows of the shelves to stay out of sight. Cooped up between two large brown boxes, I blanketed myself using a brown empty bag I had snagged from the lowest row.

"This is Doc. I'm on the ground, covering the manhole," I whispered low enough.

"Doc, get back down to the tunnel," Zarek's frustration was evident.

"We were almost outed and killed. I'm not taking chances."

"Dammit, Doc. Get back down, this is an—"

Zarek's *order* was interrupted by a loud roar followed by a massive sequence of gunfire. I heard it came from the second floor where Dylan and Logan were supposed to be.

"Gunner, Titan, come in?" I asked.

Silence.

"Gunner, Titan, sitrep," Zarek urged.

Silence followed for another few seconds. But those seconds seemed so damn long. My mind went back to the last time I had a conversation with either

Logan or Dylan. A lump formed in my throat at the thought of either of them hurt.

"This is Titan. Gunner is trapped in one of the rooms," Dylan strangled message left goosebumps through my entire body, "Icarus is on the move."

"Titan, proceed extraction without me," Logan said. He didn't sound too bad.

"On it, Gunner," Dylan responded.

"I can't locate Gunner," Amelia said calmly but a hint of terror broke through.

"I'm in the third room from the stairs, towards east. It looks like a metal cage in here," Logan growled.

"Gunner, hold your position. Oscar Mike for rescue," Zarek said panting and then, "Fuck! I'm taking fire. There's mercs converging on the south wall."

My heart sank.

"Mercs converging on the east wall. There's two loaded cars," Delara added.

"We have incoming on the north wall. Two SUVs," Kabir said.

No. No. No.

"Fuck. I think they have us surrounded. I have ten more mercs on the west wall," Sebastian said, "Ghost, Shadow and Cipher, hold position and cover. Do not let them inside. I repeat, do not let them inside."

A string of '*Copy's* sounded.

I held my breath for a few seconds and let out a heavy sigh. My heart was pounding in my ears and I couldn't think of anyone but Logan.

'I can't lose you.'

Logan.

I had to get him out before the demolition

happens.

I cleared my throat of the lump that was inevitable and rasped, "This is Doc. Permission to rescue Gunner."

There was no response.

I repeated my message, "This is Doc. I'm in pursuit to rescue Gunner, over."

Silence. A moment later a loud static noise sounded in my earpiece and I flinched. *Fuck*. Our comms are down.

I looked frantically at my surroundings. I was sure what I had to do, rescue Logan. But I knew I didn't have explicit permission.

Fuck it.

I climbed down from the five shelves and landed on the ground with a faint thud. I gave a last look at the manhole and willed it to stay undiscovered. With my rifle in tow, I strode towards the stairs.

When the aisle ended, I surveyed my path to the stairs and saw two guards surveying their surroundings. I knelt and tactfully shot the first guard, unfortunately alerting the other one. He stiffened. When I learnt he hadn't narrowed my position, I aimed at his collarbone and fired.

Two down.

I sprinted to the stairs and started my cautious climb. Once on the upper level, I noticed there were no guards watching the entry point. A few guards were incapacitated and had their wrists tied.

Thank you, Logan and Dylan.

I walked past them and headed east towards Logan. The lobby had a path going straight from the third door. Where Logan was. A guard walked out from the path, with his back towards me, and I aimed for his chest.

Another down.

I ran towards the guard and stopped at the corner awaiting any other mercs that could be manning Logan's door.

I peeked around the corner and saw no one.

The room where Logan was supposedly held had a modern lock on it. I searched the fallen guard and retrieved a key card from his front pocket.

Praying that this was the card, I swiped it. As the door made sounds and unlocked, I kept an eye out for the corridors.

The door finally opened and I saw an unarmed man dressed in Blackthorn clothing, with a tag 'Gunner'. I couldn't see his face.

Being wary of the situation, I carefully stepped closer, my rifle still aimed at him. As he raised his hands in defeat, I saw his mask move slightly.

"It's me, Leo," his voice was severely muffled and I couldn't confirm whether it really was Logan.

I tucked my rifle and raised my left hand to his forehead while my right hand clutched my rifle.

His hand mimicked mine and when it reached my forehead, we both did the same thing. We flicked each other's forehead over the helmet.

That's my Logan.

I hugged him and armed him with my M18, walking towards the stairs.

"—omms are back up," Amelia's relieved voice said.

"This is Shadow, back at rally point," Delara said.

"This is Ranger, back at rally point," Sebastian added.

"This is Cipher, back at rally," Kabir panted.

I waited for Zarek to chime in. I paused near the stairs and waited for what felt like hours.

"This is Ghost. Four mikes to detonation. Heading to rally," Zarek finally said.

I felt the familiar large presence on my back, "We need to move, Doc."

Logan's voice was ragged. I could hear the terror in his voice. I realized if we didn't make it back to the tunnel, we'd be as good as a burnt chicken wing in an oven.

As we ran back down the stairs, more mercenaries had taken charge of the locations inside the warehouse. Team 1 was gone and ready with their position, and I realized that Jerome's team didn't have a clue about the demolition.

"Icarus extracted, Titan at rally," Dylan sighed.

I figured it was time to ping the team.

"Gunner rescued. Heading to rally," I said.

"Doc, what's your position, I'll come to you," Zarek's worried voice sounded.

"Hold your position, Ghost. We're almost there."

With a heavy sigh, both Logan and I jutted out of the stairwell into the ground floor skirmish. Once we were in the visual range of the guards, we were showered with bullets from all directions.

We ducked and rolled to avoid them. I heard Logan returning fire with my gun. I did the same and hit three guards aiming our way.

With our backs touching each other, we tactfully walked towards the manhole. As we rounded the corner of the aisle, I spotted two mercenaries firing into the hole and one lying flat on the ground. I fired, taking them down, but not before Logan jerked against my back, momentarily colliding with me.

"I'm fine, keep moving," he grunted, his voice pained. More guards streamed through the other end of the aisle and I returned fire, keeping them away.

As timings go, it was horrible, when my clip emptied and I had to pause for three seconds.

Three seconds and the whole atmosphere changed.

Three seconds and suddenly, we were no longer closing in on the rally point.

Three seconds then bled into the longest minute of my life.

I was sure I heard the shot, because in that moment, I couldn't hear much else, I reckoned. A ripple of pain shot through my arm. With a slightly blurred vision, I continued switching magazines and finally had myself armed.

It was all happening so damn fast. The merc in front of me shot one more time, hitting my bulletproof vest straight in the middle and I swore all the air rushed out of my lungs. Logan's back collided with mine again, but this time it was me who jerked.

"I'm black on ammo," Logan panted.

Fuck.

I shook my head and gained control of my rifle, firing back at the bastard who shot at me twice.

I looked over my shoulder and saw Logan fighting hand-to-hand with two mercs.

"Go, go, *go*," he shouted.

If it wasn't already chaos, bullets started flying through the aisle. A few mercenaries were firing blind from behind the boxes towards us. Hearing movement, I kicked the box hard, sending it crashing into someone in the next aisle. I fired quickly, aiming to incapacitate. I turned around and shot at the one of the mercs Logan was fighting with. I constantly watched my back as I walked closer to the manhole.

"Gunner, fall back," I yelled.

He didn't respond and kept grappling. I couldn't get a good shot of the merc and risked hurting Logan. The merc was suddenly behind Logan, his arm quickly snaking Logan's neck. Merc's head was right above Logan's and I froze. I had a clear shot but it was way too familiar.

Just a bottle on his head.
Just a bottle on his head.
Just a bottle on his fucking head.

I breathed out and fired once. The merc went limp.

"Doc, Gunner, get back down," Zarek's voice was frantic.

Just as I turned a box came flying at me from the side and pinned me to the ground. Correction, a heavy box. Logan ran to me and lifted it off me, as he took more fire. I prayed the bulletproof vest held on.

I hastily ran towards the manhole, Logan behind me.

When more mercs started rolling into the aisle, he grabbed my rifle.

"I'll cover, go," he howled.

He pushed me into the hole and I was shrouded in darkness. Gunfire echoed in the tunnel and my eyes adjusted to see the team taking fire inside the tunnel as well.

Fucking fuck.

I had no gun, and was empty. I was bleeding from my arm and had a throbbing pain in my chest from the bullet that hit my vest. The adrenaline rush wasn't going to last. My ears couldn't take any more gunfire.

No, you're not going to panic.
Oh, but I was.

Strong familiar arms grabbed me and pulled me down.

"You're okay," Zarek whispered.

And then my haze broke. I frantically started chanting Logan's name. He wasn't back. The firefight in the tunnel had ceased but Logan wasn't back.

"Clear the rally point, we're going boom in T minus ten seconds," Sebastian said.

No, no *no*.

"Gunner, return to RP," Zarek shouted.

Two legs finally emerged from the manhole and I ran to it. Just as Logan was about to jump, he was pulled back ruthlessly by someone and I heard faint muffles of struggle.

Zarek grabbed my waist from behind and pulled me back away from the manhole. Arms flailing I shouted Logan's name. My chant was interrupted.

Boom.

I was thrown back from the explosions above and landed on the tunnel's ragged floor with Zarek's body covering mine. It felt as though my ear drums had burst. I couldn't hear anything but a loud beep.
I couldn't—

THIRTY-FOUR

Zarek

My ears were ringing and I let fear consume me again. Leora was lying there, unconscious and bleeding. The remnants of the blast still lingered in the air.

I looked back at the place where the manhole should've been. Nothing but a big gaping hole, concrete slabbing off. Rebars poking out of the concrete.

No Logan.

My chest constricted.

I got off Leora and moved her away from the fallen debris. Glancing towards Kabir, it didn't take long for him to understand.

He whipped out his tablet from his backpack and tapped away.

His face contorted and his brows turned with pain. He looked back at me with unsure eyes.

No.

This couldn't be happening. I strode towards him

and snatched the tablet. It showed five dots huddled together at our location. *Five*. Not six.

I zoomed out and searched a larger area. No Logan.

With trembling hands I clicked on the list of all RLM device holders.

Leora, active.
Kabir, active.
Zarek, active.
Amelia, active.
Dylan, active.

And then, the inescapable truth in cold, unfeeling text: *Logan, inactive.*

I refreshed the screen in desperation.

Logan, inactive.

He was gone. Logan was gone.

I frenetically looked around. Dylan and Amelia were swapping glances between me and Kabir. Amelia grabbed the tablet off my hands but my arm didn't move.

Delara was crouched beside Leora checking her vitals.

There were three officers that helped us in the tunnel firefight, two of whom were cuffing the mercenaries.

Sebastian was crouched beside a panting Officer Grayson who was shot in action. They were alive.

All of us were alive and moving.

Where is Logan?

I shook my head and tried recounting the last few minutes. Logan was trapped, Leora rescued him, she made it to the tunnel. Logan didn't and then the charges went off.

What did I do after that? *Fuck.*

Why couldn't I remember?

I looked at Amelia. She had Kabir's tablet in her hand.

Tablet.

RLM.

Logan, inactive.

He was gone. His heart had stopped.

"...Zarek!" Sebastian shook my shoulders. How did he get to me? Wasn't he just near Officer Grayson?

I turned around, painfully slow, and glanced at the hole in the tunnel ceiling. Flames licked the warehouse floor. I kept repeating a chant in my head so as to not forget again.

Logan is gone.

Logan is gone.

Logan is gone.

"Rivera, look at me," my unfocused eyes were suddenly filled with Sebastian's frame. His hands on my shoulders. He unclipped my helmet and took my goggles and balaclava off.

"Breathe, man," he said and I did as I was told. Suddenly, the air rushing through me cleared my vision. Was I not breathing?

Panting, I watched as Leora regained consciousness and I ran to her.

"Logan?" She asked expectantly.

My whole body trembled. I immediately pulled her into my embrace and I felt her head frantically moving.

"Where is he?" She screamed.

"Baby," I whispered in her ear, "He's—"

"No. No. No. *No!*" She cried.

She got out of my hold and stood up, swaying a

fraction as I held her.

"Find his location! We have to get him back," she said. Her voice was shaky and uncontrolled.

"Leora—"

She cut me off, "No! Kabir, find him."

Kabir looked at me, pleadingly. Suddenly, Dylan collapsed to his knees and let out a painful roar.

That's when Leora caught up to where we all were. She took off her helmet and balaclava as she ran to Amelia who had the tablet. One look and her face changed. Her eyes turned lifeless and she turned to Dylan, now crumpled and broken, then her gaze shifted to me. I couldn't bear the sorrow in her eyes and instead, watched Dylan.

He removed his helmet, holding it close to his chest in a silent tribute to the lost comrade.

✧ ✧ ✧

"Hi, I'm Logan Carlton," the man in front of me introduced himself with a grin that seemed to stretch for miles. His eyes sparkled with a hint of mischief, as if the CIA's Special Operations Group was his personal playground rather than a serious assignment.

I shook his hand, "Zarek Rivera. And this is Dylan Desmond."

Dylan nodded, his towering presence and stoic expression contrasting sharply with Logan's vivacious demeanor. Dylan and I had started a comfortable camaraderie. Despite only knowing him for a few weeks since joining the CIA, Dylan became the only person I didn't distrust. Now, with our impending deployment to Afghanistan, AD/MS had added to our troop. One Logan Carlton and a former detective, Maxton Prescott.

"What do you think they're gossiping about?" Logan pointed at Maxton and another officer who were talking and laughing.

I frowned slightly at Logan and said, "Not our business."

We were mingling at the CIA's closing dinner party in Washington DC, where formal attire and whispered secrets were the evening's main courses. Logan's gaze roamed, clearly appreciating the elegant dresses and the allure of the female associates, while Dylan remained an unmovable fortress of calm.

Logan smirked at me, "You're not a man of many words, I see. Trust me, once we're all brothers, you won't shut up about yourself. I have that effect on people." He took a sizable gulp of his drink.

I gave him a mock smile and nodded, "I'd rather get to know you first before starting on our said brotherhood. But let's focus on getting through our assignment without killing each other, shall we? I don't want any animosity amongst us."

"Animosity?" Logan's eyes widened animatedly, "Brother, we're going to be best friends."

With a wink, he excused himself, sauntering over to a lady whose arm seemed to need his immediate attention.

What a douche!

✧ ✧ ✧

We were back at the Blackthorn office. Sebastian had gone to the hospital with Officer Grayson while the rest of us hovered near the Blackthorn private clinic.

All of us were checked and Leora was understandably under observation after being shot. Dylan's gaze was fixed on some unseen point, his usual stoicism replaced by a hollow emptiness. Kabir and Amelia communicated in silent glances, a private world of shared grief. Booth stood there, with her arms crossed over her chest. Zane was downstairs in the command center, tying up our loose ends.

The doctor arrived, her expression unreadable.

"The patient is stable, awake and responsive. She needed a few stitches, but overall she's not showing any adverse physical symptoms," she looked at me then, "Which one of you is Logan? She's asking for them."

My heart constricted, a knot of dread tightening. I nodded, feeling the weight of impending reality as I stepped through the clinic's doors into her room.

Part of me worried that I'd have to recount everything to her and watch sorrow wash over her. But there was another part, a more irrational one, that hoped that Logan would suddenly appear in the doorway and save me for the twenty-first time.

She looked so small in those white sheets. The patient gown was too large on her and with her sagged shoulders, she looked helpless.

She looked up at me with those beautiful eyes and I saw the only thing I hoped to never see.

Utter devastation.

"I remember. For a second I forgot, but I remember now," she nodded to herself, "He's gone. You don't have to repeat yourself. I tried to rescue him. Fuck, I *did* rescue him. And then that ass shoved me into the manhole and let himself die anyway. I failed my rescue. I failed—"

"Leora—"

"No, I did. I failed him. I failed the squad. I couldn't fucking protect him," she continued to frantically ramble as I sat down near the foot of the bed, "I don't deserve to be a part of this squad. I failed Lo. He's gone. He's fucking gone. Poof."

A laugh rumbled in her chest and her sagged shoulders shook with hysteria. *Shit.* She's going to have a psychotic breakdown if I don't bring her back.

"Baby," I shifted closer to her and cupped her cheeks as she kept laughing, "Look at me. You didn't do this. He died protecting you. He loved you."

Something I said made her laughter snap off.

She fixed me with her piercing gaze and whispered, "Love. Do you still love me? I killed your brother. You should hate me, Zarek."

This beautiful, amazing woman, who tried to save my brother, thought she could do something to make me hate her? But all I saw in those eyes in that moment was surrender and acceptance.

"Baby, I could never hate you. But you didn't kill him. You tried to save him. You're my hero, Leora. You did something that someone in your position wouldn't have. They'd have been too scared. But you did it. You made it your mission to save Logan."

I dropped my head on hers and felt her shivers and uncontrollable sobs.

"But he died anyway," she started wailing then.

Even though Leora was falling apart, I found her vulnerability drawing mine to the surface. So, I finally let go.

With a deep breath, I surrendered to the emotions. My body trembled with sobs, and I let myself face the harrowing truth: Logan was gone.

EPILOGUE

Leora

ONE MONTH LATER

I realized that there was a limit to grief. At a particular point it was unwillingly morphed into acceptance until you're left with nothing but the memories. That happened to me one day. It was a regular day at the Blackthorn security office. Planning. Plotting. Completing smaller assignments for a bigger goal of getting to Garret motherfucking Tyson.

Jerome Tyson had given us nothing and after a week of 'questioning' by Sebastian, he killed himself with a key that some junior officer had left in his interrogation room. Who knew that if you're willing, you can find your carotid artery in four attempts.

It had been three weeks since that incident and Zarek and I were in a robotic rhythm of working and mandatory therapy. Yesterday, however, was different.

He asked if I wanted to fly to Toronto to visit my parents, and I said yes.

The moment I crossed the threshold I crumpled in my dad's arms and cried for hours. My mom got help from Zarek in the kitchen and we all had a rather solemn dinner together.

I learnt that the visit did two things for me. One, it gave me a familiar safe space to fall apart. Two, it made me realize that no matter what, grief doesn't end. It just metamorphoses into something more tolerable.

I once read that grief is like a ball in a box with a pain button on one side. Initially, the ball is large, constantly activating the button, but over time, it shrinks. The hits become less frequent, yet each impact is as sharp as ever.

"Are you planning to stay in New York, then?" my dad asked as we sat for breakfast the next morning.

I glanced at Zarek and he shrugged with one shoulder.

I swallowed my mouthful of eggs, "We're not sure where we want to operate from just yet. It seems New York is the best option for now."

My dad nodded, "Have you thought about a funeral? You said he didn't have any family."

Zarek jumped in, "We thought about it, Oliver. But we're going to have a small wake instead of a funeral. It'll be in New York. We'd love to have you if you can."

"I'm so sorry again, honey. I know he was your close friend," my mom gave Zarek a hesitant smile.

Zarek gave her a pained smile but kept his calm. I'd been observing him these past few weeks. He had been detached. He barely talked to Dylan in fears of unearthing conversations about Logan. I knew Dylan was hurting too. Every now and then, I'd find Dylan pacing in front of Logan's room in the Blackthorn building.

The squad had become uncharacteristically quiet.

✧ ✧ ✧

After breakfast, we flew back to New York in the afternoon. Amelia and Dylan had also gone back to San Diego to visit their youngest sister Iris who was two years younger than Amelia. Kabir couldn't fly back to India to visit his family since it was a long fifteen-hour flight and he feared he'd miss too much work.

So, when we arrived at the Blackthorn building, it was only Zarek, Kabir, Sebastian, Delara, Ronan, Zane, and I who gathered for an early dinner. Like the meals before, this one also hung heavy with an intolerable silence. Whenever the team would gather, Logan's absence was felt starkly and pained beyond comprehension.

After dinner, Zarek shared a look with Sebastian, receiving a quiet thumbs up in response. Leaning close, his breath caressed my ear as he whispered, "Come with me, *Mi Corazón?*"

Intrigued, I followed him to the elevator, watching as he selected the top floor.

"Are we going shopping again?" I teased, earning a soft laugh.

"Sort of," he replied, his voice hinting at a secret.

The elevator doors parted to reveal a glass covered bridge to the other Blackthorn building. We continued on to the path after entering the building and turned right, beyond which lay a rooftop garden, its fairy lights casting a soft glow. But Zarek led me first to one of two doors before the garden. With a key, he unlocked it, and I half expected an impersonal hotel space. My gaze swept over the matte gray kitchen, the cozy light gray couch facing a large TV, and a door that hinted at a bedroom beyond.

This is an apartment.

What truly caught my attention was the warmth of the place, the walls adorned with photos of our squad, my family, and Logan, each frame a snippet of our intertwined lives, making this new space feel unexpectedly like home.

I turned to Zarek, shock widening my eyes. In the dim light from the garden window, his eyes glistened.

"This is one of the four empty apartments in the building. I asked Sebastian for the best one. I don't think the room downstairs would be enough for us," Zarek gave me a smile, the one I hadn't seen in about a month.

Extending his hand, I laced my fingers through his, following him to the expansive windows. Pausing at the sliding door, he flashed a nervous smile, then guided me into the crisp New York air of the secluded rooftop garden.

In the heart of the balcony, a quaint table with two chairs beckoned, serenaded by soft tunes from a Bluetooth speaker, accompanied by chilled champagne and flutes.

I quickly realized the song was *Rose* by *Honest Men*.

Venturing deeper into the garden's embrace, I admired the coral roses bordering our secluded nook. The stone beneath my feet tested my balance, but I didn't know whether it was my three inch heels or my fluttering heart.

"Zarek, this is—" I spun around.

The sight made all the words clog in my throat. There Zarek was, kneeling, his hands holding a small blue velvet box.

"Leora, you came into my life and I knew you would throw everything I had planned into chaos. A chaos I didn't realize I would eventually embrace and begin to cherish. I fell in love with you easily, because there was no other alternative for me, baby. The fears, the uncertainties I had, flew out the window the day you asked me to kiss you," he said, gently opening the box to reveal a teardrop-shaped diamond, elegantly set on a gold band. "This ring... Logan was supposed to be here, handing it to me. He was keeping it hidden for me. I couldn't bring myself to retrieve it from his room, not until now. I found it with a note from him."

Zarek reached into his pocket, pulling out a crumpled note, and handed it to me. I opened the note's delicate folds with trembling hands.

If you're reading this, it means I'm not there to give this to you in person. Bummer, right? I had this epic suit ready and everything. Just so you know, I totally planned to object at your wedding—for the laughs, obviously. You dodged a bullet there! Look after my sister, Zarek, and don't screw it up! - LC

Laughter mixed with tears bubbled up inside me, the note so quintessentially Logan. I looked back at

Zarek and his smile melted away all my lingering pain. He was happy, and so was I.

"So, Leora 'Doc' Mateez, will you take this chaotic mess that is me to be your husband?"

I knelt in front of him, laughing with tears running down my cheeks. "Yes, baby, yes! *God* yes!"

His grin stretched wide as he slid the ring onto my finger, then he pulled me into a fervent kiss. His tongue explored mine with a hunger filled with love, need, and a touch of desperation. His hands were everywhere, one in my hair, the other drawing me close. I tipped into him, and we tumbled to the ground, still locked in our passionate embrace, our laughter mingling with our tears.

Breaking away breathlessly, I quipped, "Was our trip to Toronto just so you could ask my parents for their blessing?"

Zarek's laughter warmed the chilly night air, his nod confirming my suspicion. Playfully, I tapped his chest, then sealed our promise with another deep, loving kiss.

We were ready for our forever. And with Zarek, forever felt like a promise I couldn't wait to keep.

*Wondering what's going on with Kabir and Amelia?
Take a sneak peak into their book.*

BONUS CHAPTER

Kabir

Was there any way out of this? Could I ever fall out of love with her? This was getting annoying. Damn, why did she have to be so infuriatingly perfect? Every time she spoke, it wasn't just her words that captivated me, it was the curve of her lips, the cadence in her voice that seemed to stroke the raw edges of my nerves, soothing yet stirring something deep within.

Why the fuck did I shove her into the 'just friends' box? I've been down this road before, haven't I? Fallen hard and fast, only to be left with nothing but ashes and bitter regrets. Last time, it cost me a best friend and left me sorting through the emotional wreckage that I'm still trying to piece together.

Stupid, really, to think I could keep her at arm's length when every little thing about her pulled me in closer. The more I told myself 'just friends', the louder my heart laughed at the feeble attempt. Was there truly any escape from falling for her? Maybe not. But every time I looked at Amelia, remembering the pain from before, I convinced myself it was better this way. Safer, for both our sakes.

But goddamn, look at her.

"Are you even listening to me?" She threw her hands up in exasperation. We were in the command center, diving into work at three in the morning, as usual.

"Nope, your voice is like nails on a chalkboard, but here I am, trying to be noble." I shrugged, the corner of my mouth twitching upwards. It was way easier to poke fun at her than to blurt out: 'Amelia Desmond, you're the love of my life. Can I kiss those gorgeous lips of yours, now?'

Shut the fuck up, Kabir.

I was 99.9% sure that she felt the same way. But that 0.1% was what I clung to.

"Alright, let's buckle down," she said, cutting through my thoughts with a sharp tone. "If we reconfigure the API gateways and refresh the access tokens, it should let us penetrate the backend of the Bitch's control system. Once we're in, we can inject a reverse shell and gain admin access."

I chuckled at her attempt at hacking a high security device. "Why don't you create a technical ticket and Zane can handle that?"

She shot me a glare that could slice through steel. "Be fucking serious, Kabir. Just for once."

"Alright, alright," I conceded, half-amused by her ferocity. "But consider this—what if messing around with this thing just tips off Ling or Romano?"

"Isn't devising a workaround part of your job description?" she shot back, arms crossed.

"Fine!" I snapped my laptop open and pounded

out a series of commands. Spinning the screen towards her, I pointed to the display where Bitch was initiating unauthorized communications with a remote server.

Predictable.

"Shit! Stop it! Stop, stop, stop!" she panicked, hammering at my keyboard like it was on fire.

I barked out a laugh, enjoying the chaos a little too much. "Relax, I've blocked all outgoing pathways."

She slumped back, then shot forward to kick me sharply in the shin. "You stupid asshole! Why would you scare me like that?"

I shrugged. But before I could retract the command, Bitch began to heat up in my hands—literally.

"Seriously, Kabir," she fumed, barely catching her breath, "next time you pull something like that, at least give me a warning. I thought I was going to have a heart attack."

Her rant faded into the background as my attention zeroed in on the device growing increasingly warm in my grip. "What next? Do we try another hack?" she pressed, trying to peek at the screen.

I didn't answer right away, my gaze fixed on the Bitch as it simmered in my palm, a ticking time bomb.

I dropped the device back onto the table and sprang to my feet. Grasping Amelia's elbow, I jerked her up beside me. Hesitating, I hovered a finger near the Bitch. Even without touching it, I could feel the waves of heat radiating from it.

Instinct kicked in. In one fluid motion, I yanked Amelia aside, tackling her to the floor, and shielding her with my body.

One second passed.

Two seconds.

She looked at me, utterly stunned. "What—"

Boom.

A muffled explosion tore through the command center, and I felt shards of the Bitch pepper my back.

Lying there, my heart hammering in my chest, I realized the narrow escape. Just seconds before, Amelia had been in the direct path of potential shrapnel. If I hadn't acted… *fuck.* The realization sent a cold shiver down my spine, mixed with a surge of relief.

"Are you okay?" I asked, my voice shaking with fear.

She nodded, her face pale, words lost to her. Just then, the fire alarm shrieked into life, slicing through the tension. I scrambled to my feet and extended a hand to Amelia, pulling her up. My eyes raked through her body, looking for any wounds or bleeding. I sighed with relief when I didn't find any.

We moved to the desk where the remnants of the operation lay. The Bitch was obliterated, and my laptop was nothing more than a mangled heap of electronics. Clearly, the Bitch had a self-destruct mechanism.

"What the fuck just happened?" Zane bellowed as he stormed in.

"The Bitch blew up," I yelled back, trying to be heard over the blaring alarm.

Zane surveyed the damage, his eyes narrowing at the destroyed laptop and the absence of the Bitch. "It's completely gone?"

"You can scrape its pieces off my back?" I quipped, half-turning to show him the shrapnel wounds.

Amelia's breath hitched, and her hand flew to the small of my back, her touch sending unexpected shivers across my skin.

Zane tapped his watch, and the fire alarm abruptly ceased its wailing. "Get cleaned up," he instructed before turning his attention to salvaging the hard drive of my laptop. I wasn't overly concerned about the destruction of the Bitch; I had anticipated some level of self-defense from it. Fortunately, I had managed to upload all crucial data to the cloud before it went critical. We should be in the clear, data-wise.

Dylan and Zarek burst into the command center, their expressions thunderous.

"It was the Bitch, not me," I announced preemptively, holding up my hands as they approached.

"That's my sister, you ass!" Dylan snapped, his eyes blazing.

From beside me, I heard Amelia's stifled chuckle. "He's talking about the Crazon device, *you ass*."

Dylan's scowl morphed into a grin. "It actually blew up?"

"Must've been programmed to self-destruct," Zarek added, looking over the debris with a critical eye.

Meanwhile, Zane was deep in his task, picking through the remnants of my laptop like a surgeon. I knew he took every device casualty personally, treating his electronics like fragile babies.

I'm sorry, Zane. I'll build you a new baby.

"Come on," Amelia said, tugging at my hand. "Let's get you cleaned up. Your back looks like shit."

I couldn't suppress a grin as I followed her to my room. When we got there, she rummaged through my closet for the first aid kit.

I peeled off my t-shirt and sat on the edge of the bed, suddenly conscious of the fact that Amelia would soon be touching my back. Even though she'd be wearing gloves, the thought made my heart race.

Fuck.

As I waited, trying to steady my ragged breathing, I barely registered any pain from the wounds themselves. But the anticipation of Amelia seeing my bloodied back filled me with a different kind of discomfort. I didn't want her to see me like this, vulnerable and marked.

Then her touch came—gentle yet tentative on my upper back. "Lia," I murmured involuntarily, barely above a whisper.

"Just hold still," she said, her voice catching slightly. "This might hurt a bit. I need to get the shrapnel out."

I nodded, and she went to work. She was deft with the tweezers, her movements sure and gentle. Each contact, every breath she took close to my skin, sent shivers down my spine.

After she finished cleaning the wounds and was packing away the first aid supplies, I turned to face her. My heart clenched at the sight of her tearing up over me.

Come on, Lia. Don't fucking cry. I can't handle that.

A single tear escaped her, tracing a path down her cheek and I itched to wipe it with my thumb.

"Lia," I said, reaching out to her. "Please, don't. It's not as bad as it looks."

She busied herself with the kit, her hands shaking slightly. She was clearly trying to hide her vulnerability.

"Lia, what's wrong?" I pressed.

"It was just... a close call, that's all," she managed, not meeting my eyes.

"But we face danger all the time. What makes this different?"

She met my gaze, her eyes swimming with unshed tears, and in that moment, without warning, her lips found mine.

She's kissing me, goddamn.

It was a fleeting, desperate kiss, one that I wasn't prepared for.

Frozen, I didn't respond. As reality snapped back, I instinctively pulled away. The hurt that flashed across her face was unmistakable.

Embarrassed and rattled, she stood abruptly, her movements clumsy with haste.

"Lia, I—" I fumbled for words. "Fuck. We shouldn't—"

But she was already shaking her head, tears now freely flowing, as she dashed out the door, leaving me with a tangled mess of feelings and the echo of what might have been.

AUTHOR'S NOTE

This journey began in 2013 with a simple scene: a girl saves a stranger who turns out to be a special agent. As I daydreamed more about the scenario, plot points began to crystallize, expanding beyond my initial idea. Originally intended as a standalone story, the narrative grew in complexity and depth as I delved into the first few chapters. I found myself falling in love with the ensemble of characters, each one demanding their own story and a chance to justify their actions.

Thus, the "Squad Six" series was born—a tapestry of lives intertwined in danger, secrets, and survival. While the main couple does find their happy ending, I chose to conclude with a cliffhanger, recognizing the scale of the antagonist's plan was too vast for just one book. This wasn't just about wrapping up a single story; it was about setting the stage for a larger, more intricate narrative to unfold.

My hope is that this book resonates with women who see a bit of Leora in themselves—those looking to escape to a larger world, eager to fight their way through trauma, and in search of motivation to pursue such a path.

A question I'm often asked is who my favorite character is. Although I hold each character close to my heart, Logan has a special place among them.

Thank you for joining me on this thrilling ride. May you find a piece of yourself in these pages.

ACKNOWLEDGEMENTS

Writing a book is never a solo journey, and I am beyond grateful for the incredible people who supported me along the way.

To my amazing early readers—Prarthana Sareen, Zarah Uy, Prachi Sharma, and everyone else who was kind enough to share their honest feedback—thank you for your invaluable insights, your time, and your encouragement. You helped shape this story into what it is, and I couldn't have done it without you.

A huge thank you to my parents for their endless love, support, and patience. Your belief in me has always been my greatest source of strength.

To the wonderful people who inspired the names of my characters, knowingly or unknowingly, you've left a lasting mark on this story in the most meaningful way.

Finally, to every reader who picked up this book—thank you for joining me on this adventure. Your support means the world, and I can't wait to share more stories with you.

ABOUT THE AUTHOR

Bakul Sharma is a contemporary romance and fantasy author known for weaving complex narratives that capture the intricacies of human emotions and relationships. Her books, including the "Squad Six Series," blend intense romance with gripping suspense and action, creating stories that not only entertain but also resonate deeply with readers.

When she's not writing, Bakul enjoys kickboxing and taking care of her cat, finding balance and inspiration in these moments of action and calm.

Website: **authorbakulsharma.com**
Instagram: **@bakulsharmawrites**
TikTok: **@bakulsharmawrites**

"Mission complete, but we've got a man down. **Squad Six**, over and out."

Printed in Great Britain
by Amazon